HOUSE OF YORK

CHARLOTTE BYRD

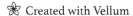 Created with Vellum

When I met Easton Bay, my perfectly ordinary life changes forever.

Captured and taken to a private island, I find myself under the thumb of a dangerous man whose **touch I crave.**

He is beautiful, damaged and tender, and **his obsession knows no limit.**

Forced into his cruel world, I must do anything to survive, even if it means **winning his hand marriage.**

"Fast-paced, dark, addictive, and compelling" - Amazon Reviewer ★★★★★

"Hot, steamy, and a great storyline." - Christine Reese ★★★★★

"My oh my....Charlotte has made me a fan for life." - JJ, Amazon Reviewer ★★★★★

"The tension and chemistry is at five alarm level." - Sharon, Amazon reviewer ★★★★★

"Hot, sexy, intriguing journey of Elli and Mr. Aiden Black. - Robin Langelier ★★★★★

"Wow. Just wow. Charlotte Byrd leaves me speechless and humble... It definitely kept me on the edge of my seat. Once you pick it up, you won't put it down." - Amazon Review ★★★★★

"Sexy, steamy and captivating!" - Charmaine, Amazon Reviewer ★★★★★

" Intrigue, lust, and great characters...what more could you ask for?!" - Dragonfly Lady ★★★★★

"An awesome book. Extremely entertaining, captivating and interesting sexy read. I could not put it down." - Kim F, Amazon Reviewer ★★★★★

"Just the absolute best story. Everything I like to read about and more. Such a great story I will read again and again. A keeper!!" - Wendy Ballard ★★★★★

"It had the perfect amount of twists and turns. I instantaneously bonded with the heroine and of course Mr. Black. YUM. It's sexy, it's sassy, it's steamy. It's everything." - Khardine Gray, Bestselling Romance Author ★★★★★

DON'T MISS OUT!

Want to be the first to know about my upcoming sales, new releases and exclusive giveaways?

Sign up for my Newsletter and join my Reader Club!

Bonus Points: Follow me on BookBub!

Standalone Novels

Debt

Offer

Unknown

Dressing Mr. Dalton

PART I
PROLOGUE - EASTON

They are not supposed to be here. They are innocent and polite and sweet. Some of them may even be kind.

They think that they are here of their own free will.

They think that it's a game.

They think that everything is going to be okay.

I know the truth.

They are not here by accident. They were all carefully chosen.

Selected.

Identified.

Vetted.

Some are here because they are gorgeous, others because they will be good at bearing children. A few are lost souls who no one will ever look for.

But some, well, they are here because of their ability to fight.

Propensity to fight.

Willingness to fight.

Not everyone wants a fighter. Not everyone wants someone to resist their every move.

But some of them do. And these are the ones who will pay the most. And to find a girl who is both beautiful and a fighter? Well, that's everything, isn't it?

Of course, there will be the ones who fail. Most will fail at least once, but some will fail for good.

We call this game a competition to keep them pacified. Calm. Quiet.

But they had all lost their freedom a long time before they ever stepped foot on the island of York.

All but one will lose their lives.

DEGREES OF FREEDOM

Freedom is difficult to describe when
you have it.

You go through life bogged down by life's little
problems. You go to work at a job you don't
particularly like.

You get paid way too little.

Thirty-four thousand dollars a year.

Your rent and monthly expenses are way
too high.

Fifteen-hundred in rent and another three-
hundred in student loan payments plus utilities. Of
course, there's the myriad of other little but not
inconsequential expenses.

The occasional lunch out.

Happy hour.

A movie once in a while.

Is this what it means to be an adult? I guess so.

After I graduated with my undergraduate degree in Psychology, I decided to work for a few years to save some money before going on to graduate school for my doctorate.

Of course, I wanted to work in the field. The only problem was that the only job I was qualified to do with just a bachelor's degree was to answer phones at a marriage therapist's office.

I scheduled appointments and dealt with the insurance companies. The job wasn't anything I ever wanted to do and I hated it.

I would sit in the freezer of an office with the zipper of my dress pants digging into my stomach, and I would feel sorry for myself. College was hard, but it was nothing in comparison to the grind of everyday life. School was broken up into semesters, and semesters into weeks, and weeks into classes and assignments. Even if a class was unbearable, as some requirements were, at least I knew when it would come to an end.

I can still remember the contempt that I felt for my job and my life, in general. Days became weeks and then months and years and everything in my life stayed the same. Clients called. Appointments were scheduled. Lunch was eaten. Money was made. Bills were paid.

But looking back now, trapped in this God-forsaken place, I would give anything to be there again.

To have that kind of freedom again.

"Number 19," a loud deep voice is piped in on the loud speaker. "It's your turn."

My heart sinks and I take a deep breath.

"I don't have all day," she says loudly.

I know what to do and I do it quickly. I pull off my tank top and take off my pajama bottoms. When the door opens, I'm completely nude. She looks me up and down.

I'm used to their glares. I don't know her name, I know her simply as C. There are twenty-six guards here. All called by different letters of the alphabet.

"Let's go," she says, leading me to the end of the hallway.

The ground is cold and wet under my bare feet. I'm ushered into a large shower room. Five others are there as well. We exchange knowing glances, but none of us dare to say a word.

We have exactly two minutes to wash our hair and bodies. After that, the water turns off automatically and the guards throw us a small hand towel to dry ourselves.

It wasn't that long ago when I worked at an office all day hating my job.

It wasn't that long ago that I thought that I didn't have any freedom.

Now, I know better.

Now, I know what real imprisonment is like.

Now, I know that the life that I hated so much before is one that I would do anything to get back to now.

After drying myself off, C leads me back to my cell. The walk back is even colder than before, but I appreciate being given the opportunity to clean myself.

"E will be in shortly," C says. "It's your turn to be shown."

My throat clenches up in fear.

To. Be. Shown.

What does that mean?

WHEN SHE GETS ME READY...

*B*eing shown.

I've heard whispers about this, but none of the prisoners really know what's going to happen. The guards? They know. Of course, they know, but they aren't talking.

When C leaves, I put my pajamas back on and sit down on the bed. I wrap my hands around my knees, resting my head on top.

I wait.

A few minutes later, E comes in. Her hair is cut short, blunt at the edges, right by her chin. Her eyes are severe, without an inkling of compassion. Her skin is pale. Her bright red lips stand in stark contrast to the gray monotone uniform that all the guards down here wear.

Besides the bright red lips, she is not wearing a smudge of any other makeup.

She lays a garment bag and a big black box on my bed.

After washing and drying her hands, she opens her makeup box. It's so large that it has wheels like a suitcase. She gets out a big spotlight and shines it in my face. There is no mirror here, so I cannot see what she is doing as she starts to apply foundation to my face. All I see are the tools. Foundation brush. Concealer brush. Eyeshadow primer. Eyeshadow brush. Highlighter. After a few minutes, I lose track of everything that she's doing.

"So...how did you get this job?" I ask. Partly out of curiosity and partly out of boredom.

I haven't talked to anyone in days and life gets tedious that way.

But E ignores me.

"You're just not going to answer me?" I ask. She gives me a little shrug. Progress.

"Are you not allowed to talk?" I ask.

"Of course, I am," she says. Apparently, I have insulted her.

"So, why don't you answer me?"

She shrugs again.

"I applied for it."

"You applied for it?"

"Did I stutter?" she asks.

Now, it's my turn to shrug.

"So...you don't live here?" I ask.

I don't really know where here is, but I hope that she can help me figure it out.

"I just work here. I live on the mainland."

Wow. There's that word.

Mainland.

How long have I been here? I'm not sure exactly. But in all that time, I didn't realize that we were on an island.

Do you know what happens here? I want to ask. Do you know that we are all prisoners? You must. Of course, you do.

I want to ask, but I don't know who I'm talking to. She's a stranger. And just because she's a woman, doesn't mean that she is necessarily on my side. She is an employee, after all.

So, I decide to ask something else instead.

"So, what does E stand for?"

"It's just a letter."

"You don't have a regular name?"

"Not here."

"Why?"

"No one here has names. Privacy reasons."

I look straight into her eyes. Is she trying to tell me something? Reach out? Or is she just stating the facts?

"My name is Everly," I say. I need to make a connection, any way I can.

"No." E shakes her head. "Your name is Number 19. And you will never mention Everly again, if you know what's good for you."

It sounds like a threat, but it's not. More like sound advice from someone who has a little sympathy for me. At least, I hope so.

If she won't tell me anything about herself or this place, then maybe she will tell me something about what is about to happen.

"Why are you here?" I ask. "Why are you doing my makeup? Dressing me up?"

"Because that's my job."

"But what's it for?"

"You are going to be shown."

"What does that mean?"

"There will be a competition. A contest with judges. Only, it won't look like a contest. Everyone will want to be there. It's a privilege just to be chosen. You will all live in a big house together. Play. Have fun. But every few days, someone will leave."

The way she says the word 'leave' sends shivers through my body.

"What do you mean by leave?"

"There will only be one winner. And the winner will get to leave with her life."

"And...go home?"

"No." E shakes her head. "You will never go home. You will be his."

"Whose?"

"I've already said too much."

"That doesn't exactly sound like a contest you'd want to win," I say after a moment.

"It's not. But it's better than the alternative."

PART II
BEFORE YORK

EVERLY

WHEN LIFE DRAGGED ON...

*I*t's almost lunchtime. I keep glancing at the clock in the waiting room. For a few moments, I blank out and watch the little hand make its way around the face of the clock.

Is this what my life is coming to?

I'm twenty-five and feel utterly lost. Scrolling through Facebook and Instagram, I look at the pictures that my friends from college are posting.

One is traveling around Scandinavia.

Another got married in Scotland.

Two more are backpacking through Australia.

Three girls who lived on my floor junior year are planning their weddings and posting a zillion updates about their great new lives.

Of course, there are those who are working as

well. But even they seem happier than I am. Here they are living it up at a club in New York. Having brunch in Miami. Sailing around Nantucket.

What do I have to post and share?

Here I am at my desk, counting down the minutes until I get out of this ice-cold office and go out to lunch.

I know that I should bring a brown bag and eat in the break area like Phillis, but I just need to get out of this place.

I can only take the fluorescent lights and answering calls with a friendly, "Dr. Morris' office. How may I help you?" for so long.

Finally, the clock strikes noon and I don't hesitate for a moment. I already have everything I need ready. I grab my purse and dash out.

If Dr. Morris would have it her way, I'd stay on and answer calls all eight hours a day. But her business partner, the office's legal counsel, insisted that even the receptionist has to have time off for lunch.

As soon as I get outside, the stiffness of the humidity is like a punch to the throat. Most people in Philadelphia wait all year for summer and then spend these precious three months complaining about the heat.

Not me.

I love it.

The heat engulfs me like a warm soft blanket, putting me immediately at ease. I take off my sweater and enjoy the sunshine on my bare arms.

The only good thing about my job is the location.

Smack in the middle of Rittenhouse Square.

It's a beautiful historic park in the middle of old Philadelphia, surrounded on all sides by tall expensive apartment buildings and a bunch of little boutiques, cafes, and cool shops on the ground level.

Having grown up in the bland suburbs, with cookie cutter malls and chain restaurants, I relish in the city life that is my life now.

But of course, it's not without its drawbacks.

For one, I can't afford to live really close to Rittenhouse Square, or anywhere particularly nice in central Philly, because I don't even get paid thirty-five thousand dollars a year.

But since I do live in the city, my rent is high in comparison to say a nice new condo that I could get further away.

I graduated from Middlebury, an exclusive liberal arts college in the middle of New England. Vermont, to be precise. Most of my friends were from wealthy families from all around the Northeast so after graduation many of them moved to New York City.

Unlike them, I took out a lot of student loans to pay for my private education. The only job offer I got that was anywhere in my intended field was at Dr. Morris' office in Philadelphia. So, I moved to Philly. It's significantly cheaper here than in New York, but by no means is it at all affordable.

I duck into my favorite coffee shop, down one of the cobblestone alleyways around the Square. The barista has spiked hair and tattoos lining her arms. She is also very good at making all different types of coffee.

Today, I opt for just an iced latte.

"Are you okay?" she asks.

For a second, I'm tempted to lie.

I could just say that I'm tired.

Fake a smile.

"Actually, no, not really. My job is really bringing me down."

"Why? What's going on?"

"Well, it's not really what I thought it would be. I mean, I know that I'm not qualified to do much with just a BA, but answering phones is just...eh. I don't know. Maybe I'm just having a bad day."

"I'm sorry about that."

"I don't want to bother you. Thanks for asking."

I grab a seat on the big plush orange couch by the window and try to put it out of my mind.

On one hand, I'm lucky to have a job at all. Lots of graduates nowadays are still looking for work with no luck. But I still can't help but hate what I do.

"Here's a muffin." The barista comes over. "I thought it would give you a pick me up. It's on the house."

"Oh, wow." I look up at her. "Thank you."

I appreciate her compassion, but I want to resist eating the muffin.

I didn't bring anything for lunch on purpose.

Today, I need to skip it. It's my punishment for eating two bags of potato chips at ten this morning after dealing with a particularly annoying married couple who kept insisting that their insurance company was supposed to cover their visit.

In addition to hating my job, I also hate the way I look. I tend to put on weight easily so eating healthy is something that's a necessity for me.

For a long time now, I've avoided looking at myself in the mirror. You know, really looking. Finally, a month ago, I gathered enough strength to step on the scale. That's when I discovered that I'd gained thirty-three pounds since graduation. Time passes a lot faster at work when I spend my days munching on snacks and candy.

Soon after, I decided to start a low-carb diet. Carbohydrates are my weakness and I definitely have mood swings in the afternoons if I don't have a generous dose of something sweet.

I've had good luck with this type of diet in the past when I only had to lose five pounds for a college formal, but this time, I'm going to have to go all out.

This time, I'm going to really commit.

At least that's what I said to myself two weeks ago.

The only problem was the execution.

I would start each day with the greatest of intentions, but one annoying client or a short comment from Dr. Morris, would send me to the vending machine for some relief.

Not surprisingly, I hadn't lost a single pound. In fact, I gained two.

I stare at the muffin and take another sip of my iced latte.

I'm going to be strong.

I'm not going to have this muffin.

What if I just have a taste? It would be rude not to.

I break off a little crumb and toss it into my mouth. The explosion of sugar awakens my taste buds. My mouth starts to salivate.

Whatever strength I had to resist only a moment ago, all but vanishes.

I eat half a muffin in no time flat.

Another minute later, the whole muffin is gone and I feel even crappier than I did before.

Shit.

Why the hell did you do that?

How can you be so weak?

I beat myself up over and over again.

Then I feel guilty for doing that.

Everyone says that you're supposed to love your body. You're supposed to appreciate it no matter what its size.

But what if you can't?

What if I don't want to be this weight?

What if I don't feel my normal self at this weight?

How can I force myself to love myself?

One thing's for sure.

What's done is done and I have to find a way to forgive myself for eating that damn thing.

"Hey there." A male voice startles me. "You mind if I sit here with you?"

EVERLY

WHEN HE ASKS ME OUT...

*H*e stands next to me and waits for my answer. I give him a brief nod and he sits down on the other end of the couch. Plopping his bag next to him, he pulls out his laptop.

"Man, it's a scorcher outside, isn't it?" he says.

I shrug. "I guess. But I don't mind it."

"You don't?" He raises his eyebrows at me. I smile.

His perfectly messy sandy blonde hair falls into his eyes in that sexy way. His bright blue eyes twinkle as he smiles.

"I actually like the heat. I get cold a lot."

"Oh, that explains that winter sweater there." He laughs and his whole face lights up.

I shrug. "I work in an icicle of an office."

"Sorry to hear that," he says and plugs his laptop into the nearest outlet. "Oh, where are my manners? I'm Jamie."

"Hi, I'm Everly." I shake his hand.

"Everly. That's such a beautiful name."

"Thanks. It's a bit unusual though," I say shyly.

I've always felt a bit uneasy about my name. It's actually going up the charts as a popular girl's name for babies now, but when I was growing up, I was the only one who had it.

In a small conformist community like the one where I grew up, it wasn't good to have anything that set you apart from the rest. It was hard to fit into a sea of Ashleys and Jessicas with a name like Everly.

"Well, I love it," he says with a coy smile. I can't help but smile back. There's something infectious about his attitude. It just puts me into a better mood.

Even though I try to put him off, we end up talking for a while. I find out that he's from a small town in New Hampshire and moved to Philly to live and take care of his grandmother. He's taking classes at Temple and is trying to be a poet.

"A poet, huh?" I ask. He nods.

"Let me guess," he says, nodding. "Your first thought is how the hell am I going to make money doing that?"

I shrug. "Actually, no. My first thought is that you must be some kind of a romantic."

"Well, I am. I love Robert Browning and Emily Dickinson. Shakespeare. Maya Angelou, of course. Dorothy Parker."

Those names bring memories of the two English courses that I took in college, which I thoroughly enjoyed.

I raise my eyebrows.

"What? You don't approve?"

"No, I'm just surprised," I say. "Not many guys like to read fiction, let alone poetry; let alone poetry by women."

"Oh, well, they're fucking missing out then," Jamie announces proudly.

"So, are you taking poetry classes at Temple?" I ask. He nods. I've had my own aspirations to write something one day, but those dreams have been squashed by the drudgery of my daily life. I want to tell him this, but I don't trust him yet.

"I love poetry, but I want to be a realist. So, I'm taking classes on short story writing as well."

"Oh, you mean as like a backup career? In case, being a poet doesn't work out?" I joke.

"Now, there's a smile!" Jamie announces. I can't help but blush. His confidence is disarming.

I look away shyly.

"Sorry, I didn't mean to embarrass you. You just have a beautiful smile."

I shake my head.

"What? What's wrong?"

"Nothing," I mumble. "I'm just not used to having anyone pay me so many compliments."

"Well, get used to it," he says, getting up. "I'm going to get something to drink. You want anything?"

"Another iced latte would be great."

As I watch him head toward the counter, I tell myself to stay calm. But thoughts just keep swirling around in my head.

What the hell are you doing, Everly?

You are over guys, remember? No more dating. At least, not for a while.

I'm very well aware of the promises that I've made myself. It had been six months since I got out of my last relationship and, after everything that he put me through, I needed a break. A good long break. I'd sworn off guys for good.

But looking at Jamie's perfectly toned ass and wide shoulders as well as his infectious personality and sweet smile, I couldn't help but notice all the ways in which he was different from Damien.

CHARLOTTE BYRD

For one thing, Damien thought that all literature was a joke.

What's the point of reading novels? It's all made up. He used to say.

When I tried to explain that the point of reading books is to put yourself into another person's experience, he would just laugh and say, *what's the fucking point?*

For some reason, he not only didn't like reading fiction, and romance in particular, but it actually irked him on some other level. He would go out of his way to put me down for reading the types of books that I liked to read.

My favorite books are the ones written by indie romance authors. You know, the ones that do it all on their own. They write the stories they want to write, they publish them, they market them.

They are the types of authors you can just reach out to on Facebook and tell them how much you loved their books and they will actually write you back. They are basically women just like me.

Well, maybe not exactly like me. They are the ones who actually have the initiative to write down the stories that swirl around in their heads.

It's embarrassing to even think about it now, but I dated Damien for close to a year. Our relationship was good, and healthy, for maybe three months, and the last nine were just a slow descent into anger and resentment.

He never supported me in anything I wanted to do. If I even had an idea for something that I would want to try to make, like baking a cake from scratch and decorating it, he would make fun of it.

Why do you want to waste your time doing that? He'd say. *You can just buy one at the store.*

It's not going to work out, you'll see. It will be a waste of an afternoon.

Frankly, I don't know why I let myself stay in that toxic relationship for that long. Talk about a waste of time.

So, after one particularly brutal and ugly fight that lasted well into the night but luckily stopped short of violence, I'd called it quits. I'd gathered everything I had in his apartment and left. This time, for good. On the way home, I'd sworn off men. Not all of them are like him, of course, but I knew that I needed to take the time to myself to figure out how to avoid this kind of a relationship in the future.

"Here, you go." Jamie comes back.

Our fingers meet as he hands me my drink, sending a shock of electricity through me.

"Thank you," I say.

We drink in silence for a moment. Oddly, comfortable silence. I've just met him and yet, I feel very much at ease. Calm. Like I've known him for a long time.

"Can I ask you something?"

"Sure."

"Do you have any plans Friday night?"

I look straight at him. Deep into his eyes. Is this a game? Or is he genuinely interested?

"No," I finally say.

"Good, because I'd like to take you out."

I take another sip without saying anything.

"Will you go out with me, Everly?"

"Yes."

*T*he decision to go out with Jamie was a split second one. But sitting here across from him in a dimly lit French restaurant, I know that it was the right one.

Sometimes, you just have to throw away your rules and take a chance on someone.

As we talk, our conversation flows naturally. I ask him about his life growing up and he asks me about mine. We get each other's references and we find out that we both love the same shows and movies.

"So, what do your parents think about you wanting to be a poet?" I ask, tapping the top of my crème brûlée. It makes a crackling sound as it bursts in two and the goodness inside oozes out.

I've decided to make this a no-guilt dinner.

There's no way I could say no to any of the delicious food on the menu, let alone the desserts.

The only thing I can do is not feel guilty about it afterward.

"Eh, they aren't pleased," he says with a shrug. "As you can imagine. They don't know anything about poetry and don't really care. My mom's a nurse and my dad's an engineer. They are very science-oriented people. Results-oriented. If you know what I mean."

"I do." I nod. "Unfortunately, I do."

I tell him that my parents were also somewhat perplexed by my decision to go to Middlebury. They didn't care that it's one of the top five liberal arts colleges in the United States. To them, Penn State was just fine.

"They just couldn't understand why I would want to take out loans to pay for 'some prissy little school' and get a useless Bachelor of Arts degree.'"

"Isn't it disappointing when your parents don't support you?"

I nod. Actually, it is. I haven't really thought of it that way before, but now that he just came out with it, that is the right word for it.

I used to write it off and rationalize their position as something that they simply didn't understand, but now I think that it's something that they just didn't want to understand.

"I think to them, Middlebury and Oberlin and other liberal arts schools like that are just for debutantes and people from high social classes. Not something that someone like me should have bothered with," I say.

"What do they do?" he asks.

"They are both insurance adjusters," I say. "They used to lecture me about how I would never fit in with those girls no matter what I did. They have rich families and will marry rich men."

One time, I made the mistake of asking them why they thought so little of me, maybe I would marry a rich man, too. The joke backfired. It resulted in a number of talks with my mother about the importance of marrying for love rather than money. But when I asked her why I couldn't choose my career based on love rather than money, her only answer was that you need security. Love doesn't pay the bills. Unless you marry a rich man, I joked, unable to resist. And a new loop in the conversation began.

"I think they just wanted me to know for sure that they would not be supporting me after I graduated," I conclude.

"I'm sorry," Jamie says, tilting his head.

"No, it's fine. I don't expect them to. Not at all. That's why I'm working now. I just wish that they were a little bit more supportive of where I went to school and what I majored in because it was important to me."

I take another bite of my dessert.

"So, you really want to get your PhD then?" he asks.

I shrug.

"Isn't that what you said?"

"I don't really know."

Those words hang in the air between us. It's the first time I've ever admitted that to myself, let alone to someone else. For two years, I have been telling everyone that all I wanted to do was save up some money, get some experience in the field, and start graduate school.

But now? Well, I'm not so sure anymore.

"The thing is, that I really don't like my job," I say.

"You're just a receptionist. I'm sure that it would be totally different to be a licensed psychologist. Therapist."

"Yeah, maybe." I shrug. "Except that I know what it means now, and I'm not sure if I can handle it."

"Really?"

"Well, the thing is, I know exactly what Dr. Morris does. I have sat in on a few sessions to take notes. It's hard. People come with all of their problems and issues. At first, it was interesting. You sort of get this inside glimpse into who people are behind the mask they wear in the outside world. But after a while, it's...tedious. Tiring. Exhausting, really."

"That sucks," Jamie says.

I shrug again. "I have no idea why I'm telling you this. This is the first time that I've even really had the courage to say any of this out loud."

"Well, that's what I'm here for," Jamie says, putting his hand on mine.

Shivers run through my body.

A jolt of electricity.

"So, if you don't pursue your studies further, what is it that you do want to do?" he asks.

I think about this for a second. I want to say something sensible. Realistic. But he just makes me feel so at ease. So comfortable and unafraid.

"I want to be a writer."

His eyes light up.

His excitement gives me a bit of a jolt. I've never

said these words out loud, and I have no idea why I have this ache to tell him.

"At least, I want to write a story," I say, trying to diminish the gravity of what I had just said.

"Don't underestimate yourself, Everly. You should. If that is what you really want to do, don't let anything or anybody stop you."

I cower a little. How can he just believe in me like this?

"You really think I can do it? You don't even know me."

Jamie leans back in his seat a little.

Then he looks me up and down.

"I think you can because you want to. If it's something that you have thought about even a little bit, if it's something that you are passionate enough about, if you love words and language and reading, then I know you can write. It may take you a bit to find your voice. To find out exactly what kind of stories you want to write, but I know you can do it. And more importantly, you should."

I smile and take his hand. I didn't realize it until this very moment how much I needed to hear that.

AT THE END of our date, Jamie walks me home. We talk and laugh all ten blocks back, with our hands intertwined.

Right when we turn onto my block, he swings me around and gives me a big kiss. His lips are soft and delicious and I can't help but kiss him back.

"Are you for real, Ms. Everly March?" he whispers in my ear, wrapping his strong arm around my shoulder. "Because I'm not sure you are."

Those words send shivers down my spine. I smile and press my lips onto his again.

When we get to my door, I ask him inside.

I love the way he looks at me and I love the way he wants me.

I want him.

And not just because I haven't had sex in a long time.

"I'd love to," he says, giving me another kiss. "But I can't."

"Oh...why?" I ask, caught a little off guard.

"I have to get back home to my grandma. I couldn't stay for longer than twenty minutes and I want this to take a lot longer than twenty minutes."

Another shock of electricity rushes through me.

"Really?" I ask, nearly melting in his arms.

"Yes, really," he whispers. "So, how about tomorrow?"

"You want to come over tomorrow?"

"Yes, I'd love to. But first, I'd like to take you as my date to this party at the Oakmont."

The Oakmont Hotel is one of the oldest and most expensive hotels in the city. The cheapest room there goes for about a grand a night.

"Who do you know that is throwing a party there?" I ask.

"Hey, I may be a poor poet, but I know a lot of fancy people," Jamie says, giving me another peck on the lips. "So, will you come?"

I shrug.

"Yes, of course."

"I'll pick you up at seven. Wear something nice," he says, pulling away from me and giving me a kiss on my hand.

A true gentleman.

A party at the Oakmont. With a man who is quickly sweeping me off my feet. This isn't real, is it?

Tomorrow, the day of the party, can't come soon enough. I spend the morning shopping, but end up settling on a black cocktail dress I have hanging in my closet. It hides all of my imperfections and actually makes me feel pretty. I bought it only a few months ago, and I'd worn it about ten times already.

When Jamie picks me up, he looks even more dashing than I remember. Big kind eyes. Shiny hair. He wraps his arms around me and gives me a kiss on the cheek.

Shivers run down my spine.

There are people out there who can tell you

every detail about their date with their spouse. Those people used to make me sick to my stomach. But now...now, I'm wondering if this is the moment that we will be telling our grandchildren about in forty years.

"You are breathtaking," Jamie says. I smile. It's nice to date a poet. That's not a sentence that's likely to escape the lips of any regular guy out there.

"You look great, too," I mumble. So much less eloquent. I know.

But I'm the girl. I'm not supposed to be the one making the compliments.

We arrive at the Oakmont ten minutes later. Jamie valets the car and escorts me inside.

I've heard of this hotel, but I've never been inside. It's old and historic, but it has been modernized with plenty of glass and elegant contemporary fixtures. Glass tables. Marble floors. A small waterfall bursts into a river, which snakes its way through the lobby.

"Wow, this place is beautiful," I whisper as we head toward the reception rooms.

As Jamie holds the door for me, I suddenly feel out of sorts. Every woman I see is dressed in a long flowing gown. My above-the-knee cocktail dress is suddenly in desperate need of pizzazz.

"Why didn't you tell me that this was a formal event?" I ask.

"I didn't know. I thought it was a cocktail party."

I glare at him.

It's not a big deal for him because men's attire is a bit of a mixed bag. Some are wearing tuxedos while others are wearing just nice pairs of pants and matching jackets.

"So, what kind of party is this?" I ask as we get in line for drinks at the bar.

"A charity event to raise money for clean water in Africa," he says, putting his hand around my waist. "I'm sorry again about the dress code. I had no idea that people were going to be this formal."

I shrug, unwilling to let him off that easy. He wraps his arm around me tighter and gives me a kiss on my neck.

"Will you forgive me?" he whispers.

I smile, unable to resist him any longer.

"I guess so," I finally cave.

After we get our drinks, Jamie excuses himself to use the bathroom and I make my way around the room. I have never been one to be good at starting conversations with strangers, but I guess this is as good a time as any to give it a try. My martini gives me just enough liquid courage to turn to the drop dead gorgeous girl next to me.

"I love your dress," I say before I even give it a good look.

What else is there to say to a complete stranger besides offering her a compliment?

"Thank you. I love your dress, too," she says methodically.

"So...it's terrible about the lack of access to clean water in some parts of the world," I say.

I feel the awkwardness in my voice, but I keep going. Luckily, she doesn't seem to notice.

"Yes, it is." She nods and sways her hips.

Her black floor-length gown shimmers with each breath. For a moment, I'm mesmerized by how all the beads move in waves around her body.

"I'm glad that the Bay Foundation is hosting this gala. They do so much good in the world. Oh, I'm Cassandra by the way."

"Everly," I say, shaking her hand.

"So....is there going to be some sort of auction or something at the end?" I ask. "I'm sorry, but this is my first time at an event like this."

"Well, it's actually a silent auction," Cassandra says. "You see those tables all around the walls. If you want any of those things, you just write down the amount you're willing to give and it will go to the highest bidder."

"Oh, wow, that's great," I say.

One of Cassandra's friends pulls her away for some dress-related emergency and I make my way to one of the closest tables.

The first item I spot is titled "Your own Learjet to use for a weekend." In the photo on the table, I find a dapper looking gentleman in his late sixties, presumably the owner, standing proudly in front of the sparkling private plane.

My mouth falls open. This auction is no joke. Right next to the jet, there's a brochure of a two-night stay at a five-star hotel in Dubai. Estimated value: $20,000. One table over, there's a seven-day cruise around Indonesia.

I stare at the offerings, dumbfounded.

This is the kind of world that I only read about in books. Are the owners of these things even real?

My thoughts go back to Jamie. How the hell did he get an invitation to this party? Is he wealthier than he is letting on? My eyes search the room for him, but in the sea of black, I don't see him.

"Hello, there," someone says with a voice as smooth as molten chocolate. "Considering bidding on that yachting weekend in Newport?"

I turn around. The man standing before me is flawless.

Dark hair.

Strong jaw.

The nose of a Roman emperor.

Luscious lips.

Almond-shaped green eyes and long eyelashes.

"Yes, that's right," I say with a coy smile. In moments of intense pressure, my sarcasm button becomes activated.

"The highest bid is probably around $100,000," I say. "So, I'd have to work two and a half years at my current job and save every penny just to match it."

I don't know why I feel the need to tell him how much I make, but sometimes the words just come out of my mouth without my control. He winks at me, clearly amused.

"I'm Easton," he says, extending his hand.

EVERLY

WHEN I MEET SOMEONE ELSE…

As I shake Easton's hand, Jamie re-appears. He wraps his arm firmly around my waist.

When I glance at him, I see the possessive expression on his face. His nostrils flare out. His eyebrows furrow.

He's jealous.

I hate that this makes me excited. But the thing is, I like Jamie. And I sort of like the fact that he doesn't want another hot guy coming around his girl. If I am, in fact, his girl. The jury is still out on that.

"Easton, this is my…friend…Jamie." I make an introduction. The word, friend, gives me a moment of pause, but no better synonym springs to mind to describe our relationship.

"Actually, I'm her date," Jamie corrects me. Well, except that one.

"I was just talking to Everly about the silent auctions here. What will you be bidding on?" Easton asks.

Jamie inhales deeply. He doesn't have the money to bid on anything. Or does he?

"I think I'm going to go for this weekend trip to Paris," Easton says, filling out the form next to the package.

"It's supposed to be a silent auction," Jamie says, pulling me closer to him. He's holding me so tightly, my ribs start to throb. I wince in pain.

"Yes, of course. But I doubt that the foundation will be against a little competition. Especially, if that makes the bid go higher."

Easton hands Jamie his pen.

"Go ahead, kid," he says, crossing his arms across his chest.

"Don't call me kid," Jamie says, grabbing Easton's pen.

"Jamie, you don't have to do this," I whisper in his ear.

"I know," he says loudly.

I watch as he makes his way around the tables, evaluating each package.

I walk up to him again, taking his arm.

"Let's just go," I whisper.

"No." Jamie pushes me away.

"You don't have the money to bid on any of this."

"You don't know anything about me," Jamie snaps.

I take a step back.

He's right. Of course, he's right. We have been on one date together. What the hell do I know? Except that the only reason he's doing any of this is to impress some guy he has known for exactly one minute. Or is it that he's trying to impress me?

I have no idea. All I know is that I don't want to stay for any of this.

"Where are you going?" Jamie grabs me just as I'm about to walk out of the ballroom. He startles me, and I almost drop my drink.

The martini sloshes out onto my hands.

"What the hell?"

"Why are you leaving?" Jamie asks. There's a strange desperation in his voice. It makes me pause.

"I didn't want to watch you bid on something you couldn't afford just to impress some rich asshole," I say.

"I wasn't."

I shrug. That's a lie. I know that's a lie.

"Listen, I don't know what's going on here, but I'm going home."

"You can't," Jamie says with a pang of desperation. Should I take that as a compliment? The martini seems to have gone to my head.

"I mean...I'm sorry," Jamie says. His voice softens quite a lot. Kindness emerges. He takes my hand in his. Gently.

"I'm sorry, I'm being so...weird," he adds. "You're right. That guy did get to me. His suit. His cuff links. His whole attitude and demeanor. He's just this walking reminder of a life that I want, but will never have."

Jamie's honesty is disarming. I've never had a guy talk to me like that. Let alone, on a second date. Quite honestly, I have never met one who was capable of that degree of introspection.

"Let's just get out of here," I say quietly. His face falls.

"I'm not cutting our date short. I just don't want to be in this room anymore."

I squeeze his hand and wrap my fingers tightly around his and his eyes light up again.

"Okay," he agrees after a moment. "But let's have another drink first."

I hesitate.

"It's on the house. Please? The bartenders make mean cocktails."

I want to resist. I do. But I cave.

Following him back to the bar, I let out a sigh of relief. Perhaps we can salvage this date after all. The truth is that I don't know the first thing about him. I have no idea how to read his reactions or his triggers.

"What can I get you, miss?" the bartender asks.

"A mojito please."

Jamie raises his eyebrows in surprise.

"Decided to pass on the vodka this time," I say.

"So, you think rum will be a better choice?"

I shrug.

"It's a summer drink. An island drink. Refreshing. Minty."

"Hey, there's no need to explain. I love a good mojito," Jamie says. His hand settles at the small of my back. When I take a sip, I feel all the tension from the evening starting to dissipate.

We find a small secluded table in the far corner of the room.

"So, why did you invite me here?" I ask. He glares at me.

"No, I didn't mean it that way," I clarify. "I was

just wondering why you were going to this event in the first place?"

"I thought it would be a nice place for a date. My professor had two tickets he couldn't use so he gave them to me."

I nod. We sit together for a while. We talk about everything and anything. His classes. My job. His writing. My desire to write. People mill all around us, laughing, tossing their hair, shaking hands. But here at our table, engulfed by darkness, we are slightly apart from the party taking place all around us.

As much as I want this moment to go on, all the alcohol that I have consumed catches up with me. I excuse myself and head to the bathroom. After completing my business, I emerge to find Easton standing outside.

"You need to leave," he says, looking up from his phone.

"What?"

He repeats himself, getting closer to me. I can feel his breath on my lips. I try to move away from him, but when I take a step backward, my shoulders collide with the wall.

"You're not safe."

"What are you talking about?" I slither against the wall to get away from him.

"Something bad is going to happen."

"You're crazy," I say, walking away from him.

"You have to believe me."

"I don't have to do anything," I say, turning around. "And who do you think you are, anyway?"

"I'm trying to protect you."

"From what, exactly?"

"Your date," Easton says.

*H*is words crash into me like waves into a cliff. A pang of anger rushes up to the surface of my skin. Who does he think he is? I stare at him in disbelief. Why is he trying to ruin this for me?

"My date is a nice guy. That's more than what I can say about you," I insist.

He's just trying to scare me, I say to myself. Get a rise out of me. Just ignore him. I should bite my tongue and get out of here, but my mouth gets the better of me.

"What the hell is your problem with Jamie, anyway? You just met him," I say.

Easton hesitates. "I can't tell you. But he's one of them."

"Who?"

"He's going to hurt you."

I shake my head. "You're just fucking with me," I say, walking away. But Easton grabs my hand.

"Don't go back in there," he hisses.

"Let me go!" I snap. "Or I'll scream."

If he's just trying to freak me out, it's working. I pause for a second before walking through the ornately-carved double doors. But can you blame me? There's a lunatic standing here scaring the shit out of me. But what if he's actually trying to protect me from something?

"Why are you doing this? Do you get some sort of high from this?"

"No, not at all," Easton says.

His demeanor changes. The stark expression on his face softens. He blinks and his eyes get less intense.

"I don't want to frighten you," he says. "I just don't know how much time you have. I can't tell you much. I just need you to run. Run home, get inside, and lock the doors and do not open them for anyone."

I shake my head. I don't believe him. Is he taking me for a fool? Or am I making the biggest mistake of my life?

"Everly, please," Easton pleads. "Please believe me."

"But my purse is in there."

"It doesn't matter."

"No, I need it to get home. How am I going to pay for a cab?"

"I'll give you money," Easton says, reaching for his wallet.

"Hey there!" someone says, putting his hand around my waist. It's Jamie. I already know him by his touch.

"You again." Jamie glares at Easton. Then he turns to me and gives me my purse. "Let's get out of here."

I take my purse and we head toward the exit.

When I turn around to look back at Easton, I see him mouth something to me.

What? I mouth back.

"Run! Run!" he whispers.

"What the hell is that guy's problem?" Jamie asks when we get outside.

It would be a lie to say that the experience did not shake me up. Jamie tries to take my hand, but I push him away. I wrap my arms around myself and try to decide what to do. It's not every day that some stranger comes up to you and says the things that

Easton had said to me. So, the question is, why would he do that? Who is he? And why would he go out of his way to convince me that I'm in danger if, in fact, I'm not?

The truth is that I don't actually know anything about Jamie. Maybe he is someone dangerous. Maybe I should stay away from him. But should I believe some stranger I just met over this guy who, by all accounts, is totally normal?

I know Easton even less than I know Jamie. Can I believe him?

"So, do you want to come over to my place?" Jamie asks.

I shrug. "Actually, I don't feel very good. I think I'm going to go home."

"What did Easton say to you?" Jamie demands. His eyes turn into little beads, sending shivers down my spine.

"Nothing," I mumble.

"I don't believe that."

The little hairs on the back of my neck tell me to get away from him. But how? I have to appease him first. Make him believe me.

"Don't get upset," I say as sweetly as I can.

"So, why won't you tell me what he said to you?"

I shrug. My mind goes blank. I need an answer.

"He was just coming on to me. That's it," I say, taking Jamie's arm. I don't want to touch him, but I force myself to. I want to make nice so he doesn't follow me home.

"Okay, I'll give you a ride."

A taxi pulls up to the curb to wait for guests who might need one. I see my opportunity.

"Actually, I'm just going to take a cab," I say and open the door and climb in. He tries to get in with me, but I stop him.

"Listen, I had a great time, but I really just want to go home," I say. "I'm really tired. Besides, your car is here."

"What the hell did that guy say to you?" Jamie asks. "You can't believe him. He's got it out for me."

That's the first thing that I've heard that actually starts to put the pieces of what happened tonight together. I put my index finger up to the cab driver to give me a second.

"Why?" I ask.

"Because...he knows me. I didn't want to tell you this since I just met you. But I slept with his girlfriend. So, now he's out there sabotaging my life."

I glance up at Jamie, evaluating his facial expression. His eyebrows are raised. His eyes are wide open. He's either a very good liar or he's telling the truth.

"Okay," I say, still undecided.

"Everly, you have to believe me."

"I do," I say. "But I'm still tired and I'd like to go home. I'll call you tomorrow."

I close the door to the cab. I have no idea if I will in fact call him tomorrow, but that's not something that I have any intention of deciding tonight. I give the driver my address and lean back in the seat.

Suddenly, I start to feel sick to my stomach. My head starts to spin. I only had two drinks. It can't be from the alcohol, can it? I roll down the window to get some air, but it doesn't help. A moment later, everything turns to black.

WHEN I WAKE UP...

When I open my eyes, I'm confronted with the worst headache of my life.

A migraine? Perhaps.

I've never had one before. But my head is pounding so hard, I can barely open my eyes. I put my hand up to shield myself from the light streaming through the window.

Through my fingers, I look around the room. Vertical blinds. Beige walls. White wall-to-wall carpet. A large dresser with a mirror on the opposite side of the room. Two framed pictures of tulips in black and white hanging on the wall.

My eyes adjust a bit, but the headache doesn't subside. I get off the large king-size bed and walk around the room. The carpet feels nice under my bare feet. I open the dresser. It's filled with clothes. Each garment is folded nicely and put away. There are two doors leading from the room. One is open and I take a step past it. It leads to a large walk-in closet, a spacious bathtub, and a walk-in shower. On the opposite end of the bathroom are Jack and Jill sinks. I glance at myself in the mirror.

Wow. What a mess.

I'm wearing the same clothes I wore that night. My prized cocktail dress is wrinkled. There's a large tear down its side. My hair has crusty old hair spray in it, which makes it stick out in all directions. My makeup is smeared, giving me the eyes of a raccoon.

After washing my face, I open the drawers under the vanity. It's stocked with everything I could ever need. All the basics are there and then some.

Toilet paper.

Makeup remover.

Shampoo.

Conditioner.

Body wash.

Face moisturizer. Body moisturizer. Hand moisturizer.

Ear cleaners.

A $200 hair dryer.

$150 hair straightener.

Dry shampoo.

Body spray.

Five different kinds of deodorant.

And a large case full of enough makeup to make any Sephora-addict jealous.

"What is this place?" I whisper.

Between the bedroom and the bathroom, there's a walk-in closet about the size of my bedroom back home. Elegant wooden hangers house dresses, blouses, pants, and jeans. All in my size. Underneath the hanging clothes, I see an array of shoes for all occasions.

Flats.

High heels.

Boots.

Flip-flops.

Again, all are in my size and most are according to my taste.

Where the hell am I?

I run out of the closet and toward the other door. This is the way out. I need to leave this room if I want any answers.

I grab the doorknob. But it doesn't turn. Not one bit.

It's locked.

I knock on the door. Then I pound. Why the hell is it locked?

My breath quickens. My chest seizes up. How did I get myself locked away here?

I run over to the window and open the blinds.

Bright green foliage welcomes me from the other side. Lush ferns. Tall palm trees. Elegant pine trees. The sky is the color of the ocean. A few clouds are gathering somewhere in the distance.

Where is this? I press my face against the window for a better look. Then I try to open it.

It looks like a normal window, the kind that slides up, but after a closer examination, I see that it's far from it.

It's all a facade.

The knob at the top is nothing but a decoration. The window itself is made of thick impenetrable plexiglass.

I pound on the door again and yell for help. But it's so thick, my cries just reverberate back into the room.

I start to feel sick to my stomach. Claustrophobia is setting in. I need to get out of here. On the other end of the room, there's a small writing table and a chair. Without giving it any more thought, I grab the chair and throw it against the window. But instead of shattering it, it just bounces back at me, hitting me in the shoulder.

"Oh my God!" I fall to the floor and whimper.

What is this place? I ask myself over and over again. As my anger mixes with pity and sorrow, tears start to rush down my face.

I HAVE no sense of time here. There's no clock and there's no electronics. My only inkling of the fact that time passes at all is that my tears dry and my stomach starts to rumble. I quench some of my hunger with water from the sink. It soothes my dry mouth and clears my head for a moment. Sitting on the edge of the bed, I search my mind for answers.

The last thing I remember is saying goodbye to Jamie. I told him that I wanted to go home and I got into a cab. By myself. Right? Isn't that what happened?

Yes, I decide. I remember that firmly. Then what happened in the cab? Oh, yes, of course, I started to feel sick. Nauseated. And then...nothing. That's all. Then I woke up here.

So, does this mean that Easton was right? Is this what he was trying to warn me about?

If so, then why didn't he just come out and tell me? Why did he have to be so cryptic about everything?

Or what if Easton was the perpetrator? What if this was nothing but a ruse to get me away from Jamie?

Hot tears continue to stream down my face. I don't know what else to do but to climb into bed and under the covers. I do the only thing I can. Shut out the world in hopes of shutting off my mind.

"WAKE UP! WAKE UP!" A loud voice and louder knock startles me from my deep sleep.

Dazed, I stumble as I get out of bed and run toward the door. "Help! Help me!" I pound on the door.

"Get back," the woman's voice instructs. "Sit on the edge of the bed."

Who is she to tell me what to do?

"I am," I lie.

"I can see you, you stupid girl. Now, do as I say."

See me! My heart sinks. I look around the room for cameras.

"You won't see them," she says. "But they're everywhere. Trust me."

I walk over to the bed and sit down.

A loud unlocking sound startles me. A moment later, the door with an old-fashioned knob, which I tried to open by turning, slides all the way to one side. As it disappears into the wall, I see that it's about ten inches thick. No wonder I couldn't open it and my yells for help just echoed around the room.

"Welcome to York."

PART III
WELCOME TO YORK

EVERLY

A WARNING...

The woman standing before me is in her late thirties or early forties with short dark hair and flawless makeup. She is dressed in a tight cocktail dress and four-inch high-heel boots.

"What's going on here?" I demand to know and rise to my feet. But the woman shows me a small object, which looks like a pen, and presses one end of it.

"Please sit," she says quietly. "I will explain everything, but if you do not sit, I will be forced to use this on you."

She presses on one end and the other end lights up.

"Do not be deceived by the size of this taser. It is very small, but very painful."

I sit back down.

"Now, that's a good girl," she says. "Now, let me introduce myself. I'm M."

"Em? Like Emma?"

"No, M like the letter. All the guards go by letters of the alphabet. And all the prisoners...contestants... go by numbers."

She misspoke. Prisoners? Contestants? What does that mean?

"I'm a prisoner?"

"You are a contestant. It's a privilege to be invited to participate in this event."

"Yes, I can see that by the lock on the door. And the plexiglass window. I'm honored."

"Don't be sassy," M says. "It's not becoming and it won't get you far in this competition."

I inhale deeply. And wait.

M reaches back for a cart. It has been there this whole time, but I somehow missed it.

"I brought you food," she says. She pushes the cart inside my room.

"I'm not hungry," I lie.

"Yes, you are."

I shake my head.

"If you want to do something to pass the time, there are DVDs and books in the lower drawers of the dresser. You'll find a fully-loaded Kindle there with a big variety of books as well as paperbacks. The TV with the DVD player is here." She pushes a button somewhere on the dresser and a big flat-screen television comes out of the wall. "If you want something specific to read or watch, let me know. I will be back in a few hours to get the tray. We can put an order in for you."

I shake my head. "What is going on? Why am I here?"

"If you want to write or draw something, there are pens, pencils, and paper in the desk. Again, if you want any special supplies like oil paint, water color supplies, or an easel, just let me know."

"How long am I going to be here?" I ask. Why isn't she answering any of my questions? Is this some sort of joke?

"You are keeping me captive. That's illegal, you know." I change tactics.

"Not for the people who are doing it."

"What?" I'm taken aback by her statement.

"I'm sorry I can't answer your questions. All I can say is that you will not find any friends here. Your only way out is to fully participate in everything."

"What do you mean?"

"Try to win the competition."

"What competition?"

"For the love of a man."

My head is starting to spin from all the cryptic answers.

"Who is he?" I ask.

"It doesn't matter."

"It matters to me."

"He is looking for a new wife. It doesn't matter if you do not want to marry him. If you want to survive, you will compete and you will win."

"I don't understand," I mumble. She's speaking in English, but none of this makes any sense.

"All the contestants have been specially chosen. Selected. You caught the eye of someone special and you made it through the initial rounds of competition."

"I didn't enter any competition to get here."

"In the initial rounds, you are evaluated without your knowledge. If you pass the tests, you move on."

"So, no one cares that I don't want to be here?"

"No," M says emphatically. "You will want to be here later. Trust me."

"I wouldn't bet on it."

M leans in closer to me. Her facial expression turns grave. "You do not want to be eliminated. Trust me."

I furrow my brow. "Why? What will happen?"

"I'm not at liberty to say."

I inhale deeply. M doesn't exactly put me at ease, but in this moment, I know that she's not lying.

"I will be back in a few hours for the cart."

I nod.

"And one more thing," she says, before pressing the button to close the door. I look up at her.

"You may have a visitor or two besides me. It is in your best interest to go along with whatever they want you to do. They'll make you do it anyway, but it will be much more painful."

"What are you talking about?" I ask.

"Visitors. Men. Do not reject them. And do not consider putting up a fight. They will make you pay for it."

My heart drops. My hands turn to ice. What kind of place is this?

The door slams shut and I'm left alone with my thoughts. My heart starts to race and no matter what I do, I can't put myself at ease.

Who is going to come to visit me?

What are they going to do with me?

Will they want me to have sex with them?

I have to prepare myself, I decide. I reach for the cart and look at the food that M left. A couple of sandwiches and a big salad. I don't feel hungry anymore, but I force myself to eat some bread and the salad. The sight of meat makes me sick to my stomach. There's another loaf of bread on the table, and I take big feverish bites of it as well.

I tend to eat when I'm nervous and that's exactly what I'm doing now. As I swallow, I try to formulate a plan.

What am I going to do when someone comes to my room?

Am I going to follow her advice or am I going to resist?

I pour myself a cup of tea from the kettle I find on the tray and go to the dresser. In the drawers underneath the clothes, I find the books and the DVDs that M told me about. Plenty of entertainment. It's bad enough being here, locked in by strangers, waiting for some unknown competition that I'm supposed to win. With a dubious prize, mind you. The opportunity to be someone's wife? Some asshole whom I've never met.

But all of those things are abstract worries right now. Instead, what is freaking me out is the stranger who might walk up to this room.

What will he want?

What will I have to do?

What will happen if I don't?

I run to the bathroom and throw up. Afterward, I flush the toilet and wash my hands. When I come out of the bathroom, I see him. The door is locked. He's lying on my bed with his muddy boots on top of the bedspread. He has long stringy hair and a big scar all the way across his face.

"Well, hello there," he says.

EVERLY

WHEN I HAVE A VISITOR...

So soon? What is he doing here so soon? A lump forms in the back of my throat. I'm not ready for this. I need more time. I can't deal with this now. My legs feel like they are about to give out. I steady myself by leaning on the dresser.

"Don't be afraid," he says, crossing and uncrossing his legs.

"Who...who are you?" I mumble under my breath.

"You can call me Abbott."

"What are you doing here?"

"What do you think?"

He runs his hand across his scar and licks his lips.

"What is this place?"

"Your hell. My heaven."

"Why am I here?"

He shrugs. "For our entertainment."

Abbott rises from the bed. He walks slowly toward me. My eyes dart away from him in search of a way out. I make a run for the door.

It's futile.

I know that even before I reach the doorknob. I tried it before. But it's fake. The whole door slides with the push of a button.

"Didn't M explain things to you?" Abbott asks, grabbing my shoulders. A strong smell of liquor and stale cigarette smoke engulfs me.

"Do you really want to fight me?"

I don't. I'm not a fighter. In school, I couldn't even argue with another person without feeling sick to my stomach. Conflict is not my thing.

He runs his fingers down my arm.

"Get away from me."

"Now, c'mon, Everly. Don't make this harder than it has to be. You will be mine whether you fight me or not."

I peer into his dead eyes and know that he is telling the truth. This is not his first time. Perhaps, not even his tenth.

"Why do you want to do this?" I ask.

"Because you're pretty. And you don't want me to."

My chest seizes up. I take a step away from him. He takes a bigger one closer to me.

He runs his fingers down my neck and cups my breast. I push him away, so he returns but this time squeezes it so hard that I wince.

"Don't fight," he says. "Or actually, maybe it will be more fun if you fight."

The twinkle in his eye scares me.

I try to get away from him, but he grabs my arm and pulls me closer to him. He then presses his lips onto mine, so hard that our teeth collide.

The pain triggers something in me. Something I didn't know existed.

I open my mouth and bite down on his upper lip until I taste iron. It's blood.

His blood.

"You bitch!" He starts to say, but I knee him in the balls. Hard.

One swift motion and he's down on his knees before me.

Shocked by my own power, I take a step back. I've never hit anyone before. Let alone done any of this. Where did this come from?

"You cunt!" he screams.

Again, something else takes over my body.

I run over to the desk and grab the chair that left a dark bruise on my shoulder. When Abbott climbs up to his feet, he lunges at me. Grabbing onto the legs of the chair, I swing my body from one side to another for maximum effect.

Boom!

The chair makes a loud crackling sound as it collides with his head.

Abbott falls to the floor. His body goes limp.

I back away and search the desk for something that could be used as a weapon. I grab a pen and grasp it tightly in my fist.

Abbott still doesn't move. Blood starts to pool under his head.

I look down at my hands. They are shaking and the tremors are spreading throughout my body. My mind races.

What if he doesn't wake up? Or worse yet, what if he does?

I wait.

A few minutes pass. He still doesn't wake up.

I let out a little sigh of relief and then take a few deep breaths to try to figure out what to do. I need to get out of this room.

If Abbott let himself in, then he was planning on

letting himself out. And for that he would need some sort of button. But where? I search the walls for something, but can't find anything.

Then something occurs to me.

What if it was on him? Like a remote control?

I glance back at his lifeless body lying on the floor. I need to search him. But I don't want to touch him.

I have no idea if he's actually dead. He may just be passed out. And if he wakes up? Then what? Fear throws my body into a cold sweat.

Of course, I could kill him. He's lying there lifeless before me. Why not just finish him off? If he wakes up, I'm sure he would have no qualms about doing the same to me, prior to doing something a lot worse first.

I grab a pen from the desk and kneel over him. With one swift motion, I can lunge it into his chest or into his carotid artery. I try to make myself do it. But I can't. I'm not the monster that he is.

Instead, I search his clothes for something that resembles a remote control. I have no idea if this is even something I should be looking for, but it's the only idea I have. I don't find a thing.

So, how the hell was he going to get out of this room after he was done with me?

Before I can come up with an answer, something tightens around my ankles and pulls my legs out from under me. I fall to the floor.

When I land, the wind gets knocked out of me and I can't take a full breath. My vision fades and then turns to black.

When it returns, all I see is a large ugly scar. Something heavy is pressing me to the floor, pinning my arms back and spreading my legs open. My hands are falling asleep from the weight. I'm still struggling to take one breath.

"Get off her," someone says. When he doesn't, they pull him off me.

"No, let me get a go at her!" Abbott roars.

"You are bleeding from your head. Severely. You need to see a medic."

"Not until after I'm done with her." He punches me in my stomach and across my face. I double over in pain. This time, the blood I taste belongs to me.

"Get him off her."

Two guards pull Abbott away from me. A tall man dressed in an elegant suit kneels over me.

"You shouldn't have done that."

"What?" I ask.

"He likes his revenge. And he takes his time with it."

Shivers run down my spine.

"You should've listened to M."

I pull myself to my feet and pull my shoulders back.

"This place will break you. It has broken women much stronger than you," the guard says. "This is York."

I narrow my eyes and don't look away.

"Take her to the dungeon," he says to the other guards. "If she doesn't want to act civilized, we will show her just how uncivilized we can be."

WHERE DARKNESS HAS NO LIGHT...

*T*ears start to gather behind my eyes, but I don't dare let them out. The guards take each of my arms and escort me out of the room. My legs refuse to move, so they half drag me down the hallway.

The hallway is painted taupe. The carpet is thick and dense and the walls are decorated with paintings of serene scenes of ocean waves and palm trees. By all accounts, it looks just like a hotel hallway. Even with keyless entry doors.

The guards drag me onto the elevator and press the lowest button on the panel.

"You should not have fought him." The left one laughs. "I have no idea why some of you do that. You don't know how easy you had it."

"Fuck you," I say.

"That's not going to help either."

"Your life upstairs was a dream in comparison to what's going to happen," the other one adds. "But you'll soon see that."

I shake my head and try to stand up on my own two feet. Their hands are pressing so hard into my arms that I wince from the pain.

Once the doors open, the look of everything changes completely. No more carpet or paintings. It's dark and menacing with only a few fluorescent lights illuminating the way. The doors are stainless steel and there are thick bars on the windows.

They lead me to one of the cells at the end of the hallway. One of the guards presses his hand against the screen on the wall. After it scans his fingerprints, the door slides open.

"You never had a chance upstairs," he says. "There are cameras everywhere. Someone is always watching. In your old room. In the shower. In the bathroom. In these cells. Everyone knows what's going on here and everyone is okay with it. You will not find any friends here."

There's that statement again. No friends. That's exactly what M said.

He leads me into a large black room, which

smells like a wet dog. The floor is soaked and I slip as he leads me to the wall.

That's when I see them.

Girls.

Most are naked.

All are chained to the wall.

By their necks.

The fear in their eyes makes my instincts kick in.

No, no, no. This is *not* happening to me.

I push one guard away and kick the other.

But one zap of their electric pen and I fall to the floor. My limbs become strangers to me.

I watch as the guards drag me to the wall and put a large metal cuff around my neck. It's chained to the wall.

When I regain sensation in my body, I realize that I can't move more than a few feet in either direction.

The metal cuff sits heavy on my shoulders. There's nowhere to go. The guards leave as women around me yell obscenities at them.

Their words are foreign, all in different languages, but I feel the hatred spewing from their lips.

And then, somewhere in the distance, there are those who whimper. And some who cry.

* * *

As the guards leave, a group of men dressed in suits walk in. They walk around the room and point to certain women. Those women shake their heads and plead no.

I dig my fingers into the metal around my neck.

The men gather around the first one and start to do unspeakable things to her. Tears run down my face as others yelp wildly to get them to stop. But the sounds of anguish just make them even more excited. Once they are done with the first one, they move on to the one next to her.

"You have fresh meat there," one of the guards says, pointing to me.

The men laugh. A moment later, they are crowding around me.

Fear overtakes me and I melt onto the floor.

I slap but they slap harder. I kick but they kick harder.

There's no way to fight.

When they sense my defeat, they come closer. I close my eyes and take myself away. It's the only way to escape.

I'm standing on the edge of the ocean.

Warm water caresses my feet.

The sky is blue and the sun is bright. There isn't another human soul anywhere in sight.

A little fish with yellow and black stripes swims over to me and waves its tail.

I reach to touch her, but she swims away.

I take a few steps into the water. Then a few more.

I feel the sensation of water engulfing me.

A few more steps and I'm in up to my shoulders.

The heaviness of the chain down my back vanishes.

One more step and I will be completely under water.

I would give anything to descend into this crystal blue heaven and disappear forever.

Away from evil.

Away from hate.

Away from pain.

As everything around me turns to black, I keep reaching for the light.

WHEN THERE'S NOTHING BUT
DARKNESS...

*C*ommunication is a problem.

None of the girls here speak English and I don't speak anything else. I took Spanish for two years in high school, but I don't know enough to learn anything significant. I wrap my hands around my knees and sit in silence like everyone else.

A few girls speak to each other in hushed tones, but everyone else just stares into space. The lucky ones sleep.

How long have they been here?

How long will I be here?

Is this it now? Is this my life?

I thought that I couldn't tell time upstairs in the room, but I definitely can't tell time here. The only things that break up the day are two bowls of food, water, and men. They come in packs of two or three, sometimes more.

They speak different languages, but they always wear suits and expensive watches.

Sometimes they know exactly who they want. Other times, they pick girls at random.

I get picked a lot. They know what happened to Abbott and they are making amends. Avenging him.

But I'm getting good at checking out. I'm getting good at not being here.

I no longer fight because there is no point. Instead, I let my mind wander and drift away. They think I'm being compliant. Some of them like that. Others want to see the girl who did that to Abbott.

I feel myself becoming a zombie.

Here, but not here.

Present and yet not.

This is not happening to me because I am not here to experience it.

I'm walking in the clear blue waters.

I am running my fingers through the white sand.

I am dancing in the warm tropical rain.

Hours blur into days and days into weeks. I've counted until eleven and then I lost track. Now, I have no idea. Most of the girls are just as despondent as I am. We look at, but barely acknowledge each other anymore.

Maybe this is all that my life will ever be.

But what about the contest? The competition? Is that why they brought me here? What happened to that?

I want to ask someone about that. But who? And do I even have the energy to try?

Starving, thirsty, and tired, I sit against the wall and close my eyes. If I had the opportunity, I would kill myself. I can't deal with this anymore. Just give me the chance.

MORE TIME PASSES. More girls arrive. Terrified and loud just like I was.

More men come to do bad deeds.

I find myself checking out more and more. Reality is too hard to handle.

As I drift away, I lose myself in my fantasies.

My imagination is my only weapon. It's my only escape.

And then things get worse.

It happens all of the sudden. Without warning. She dies.

Small and frail, she has been coughing for many nights in a row. Sick from the horrible conditions. Sick from all the torture. Sick from a life underground.

Her body gives out. When a new group of men arrive and choose her, one of them realizes that she's not just pretending to be lifeless. She really is gone.

The guards take her body away, and the men continue as if nothing happened.

That's when something inside of me snaps.

Living in my imagination, pretending to be somewhere else, alleviates my pain temporarily. But it's not a solution. Far from it.

No, I can't spend my days in a daze. If I'm going to be here, I have to summon the strength to fight. If I want to survive, I have to look for a way out.

That girl had red hair, freckles, innocent eyes, and a broken heart. They took all hope from her. No one can live without hope.

That's not going to be me.

I will not let darkness take me.

I will fight with every strength I have against the dying of the light.

BUT TO FIGHT the men directly is futile. There are too many of them. I am chained. No, there's nothing to do but give in. But there are other ways to fight. I need answers to my questions. I need knowledge.

I need to know what this place is.

Where it is.

Who these people are.

I don't know what I don't know, but every scrap of information I can put together will give me the armor to protect myself and, maybe, eventually free myself.

First thing's first. I need to speak to someone.

I search my brain for any words in Spanish that I can remember. I cobble them together into a sentence.

Then I say them out loud. Loudly.

No one responds.

"How long have you been here?" I follow up my more than broken Spanish question with the translated English.

"When did you come here?" I simplify the question in English.

No one responds.

"Everly," I say, pointing to myself. "You?"

The girl next to me repeats my name, "Everly," and then points to herself. "Esme."

The next one does the same thing. After a few rounds, everyone can say everyone else's name.

It doesn't seem like much. But it's also everything.

We are no longer sitting in silence. We are no longer pretending not to see.

We have tried to keep our humiliation to ourselves, but that just made the attackers stronger. That's all changed now.

I repeat the process with my last name.

"Everly March," I say my name, pointing to myself. I repeat my name a few times and on the third time, everyone is saying it along with me. I turn to Esme.

She smiles. Wide toothy. Surprisingly, white.

"Esme Moreno," she says. We all repeat her name just as we all repeated my name.

We are making connections.

Esme Moreno. Acosta Pimco, Kacha Sonjai. The list goes on. Everyone repeats every name and every name is attached to a face. We may not speak each other's languages, but we know who we are. By the end, I know thirty-one names. And thirty-one women know mine.

The experience seems to empower everyone. We are no longer strangers. Suddenly, everyone starts to try to talk at once. The ones who know each other's languages a little bit talk the loudest. Others try to communicate using their fingers.

"How long have you been here?" I ask again. Loudly. I'm pretty sure that I'm not asking this correctly in Spanish so I repeat myself in English.

"Me?" I point to myself. "A month, I think."

They stare at me.

Month is mes in Spanish.

"Uno mes," I say. I add a shrug since I can't be sure.

A lightbulb goes off. The ones who know Spanish make their estimations. Fingers go up to make sure nothing is lost in the numbers.

Two months. Six months. Seven. Seven. Fourteen.

My heart drops. Too long. Way too long. Perhaps, this is it. Perhaps, we will all be here until we die.

EVERLY

A GLIMPSE OF LIGHT…

*I*t's difficult to make sense of a place that's nonsensical. Regular rules don't apply here. Wherever here is, after all.

York.

When the guards whisper the name, I can smell their fear. What are they afraid of?

Others use it proudly. They wear it like a coat of armor.

I have one experience of York. It's a terrible, horrific place from which I yearn to escape.

Yet, I know that there must be another. Otherwise, why would all those men be so proud?

The next time that the guards come down with food, they arrive with M. I recognize her immediately, but I cower in her presence. She takes one look at me and shakes her head.

"You do not belong here," she says. Her gold hoop earrings twinkle under the fluorescent lights. Her lipstick is bright red and her hair is razor-sharp with a professional blow-dry.

"None of these women belong here," I say.

M shakes her head.

"I warned you."

"He attacked me."

I cannot say that I don't regret what I did to Abbott. In retrospect, perhaps I should've given in. It was just him. There was no dungeon. No groups of men. But the darkness was still there.

I shake my head. No, I can't think like that. That place only had the illusion of civility. When in reality, there was nothing close to it. I was locked away in a cell. Yes, I had a bedspread, carpeting, and a bathroom. But there were cameras. Locked windows and doors. The expectation to do as I was told.

That place is no different from this place. There are shades of difference without a distinction.

But I know better than to say any of this out loud.

M peers into my eyes. She is looking for something.

"What are you doing here, M?" I ask.

"They are going to give you another chance."

I furrow my brow.

"You remember the girl who died a few days ago? They found her body right in front of you," M says. "I saw the fear in your eyes. The horror."

I nod.

"That's how everyone leaves this place. The dungeons of York."

Dungeons. Plural. Is this not the only one?

I shake my head in disbelief. The girls around me listen to what we're saying. They hear, but don't understand.

"We are all slaves, Everly," she whispers. "But we are not all slaves the way women in the dungeons are."

I shudder.

"You attacked Abbott York. He doesn't look like much, but he is the son of the King. You gave him a serious concussion and he wants you dead. Or worse."

"So, why am I alive?"

"Because he wants his revenge."

I feel tears welling up at the back of my throat.

"I think he got it," I say, shaking my head.

"I think so, too. But he doesn't."

What more can they do that they haven't done already?

"The King has been watching what you have gone through here. And how you have responded. And he is intrigued. To say the least."

"Why?"

"Because others would have broken long ago. Others have. You were chosen for the competition. You were never intended to be sent to the dungeon. The women who are sent here are from a different stock."

"Different stock? What does that mean?" I ask.

She shakes her head. "You ask too many questions. I have said more than enough."

I glare at her.

"Well, thanks for coming, I guess," I say.

"You don't sound very appreciative."

I shrug. For a crumb of sympathy? No, I'm not too appreciative. I'm about to say these words out loud, but I bite my tongue.

"So, the King is intrigued by me. What does he want then?" I ask.

"He wants you back in the contest."

She sends a signal to the guards and they remove the metal cuff from my throat. I look around at the faces in the room. Their eyes grow big. Wide. They plead with mine. I shrug my shoulders. I want to give them hope, but I don't know what's about to happen.

When they lead me out of the dungeon, the girls cheer. We have not exchanged one coherent sentence, but I consider them my friends. Their names are tattooed into my mind.

"No one has ever left the dungeon alive before, Everly," M whispers in my ear. "You should consider yourself very lucky."

I inhale deeply and let out a big sigh of relief. And yet, my heart breaks for them. All those I'm leaving behind. I don't know what will become of me, but I make a promise to myself. If I ever get out of this place, I will do everything in my power to free them.

A NEW BEGINNING…

M takes me a few floors up and leads me to a large shower room. She gives me shampoo and conditioner and waits as I wash my hair and body. After all that time of sitting in my own filth, fresh water running down my body feels like heaven. After I'm done, she hands me a towel and I dry myself off.

"You lost weight," she remarks. It's hard not to, I think to myself. "The King will be pleased."

M HANDS ME NEW UNDERWEAR, a long sleeve shirt, and a pair of pants. They look like hospital scrubs and feel just as comfortable. Following her down the hallway, I revel in my new clothes' warmth and softness.

M scans her palm and lets me inside the room on the far end. Inside the cell, I find a twin bed with fresh linens, a small pillow, and a thick blanket. On the opposite wall, there's a toilet with a sink. A desk and a chair that's bolted to the floor sits in the middle. On the corner of the desk, there are some books and a couple of pens.

"Do not think of doing anything to yourself in here," M says. "If you do, they will take you back there and, this time, you'll never get out."

I nod.

"There are cameras everywhere. They are always watching. If you try anything, they will know and they will stop you before you get the chance to... complete it. And then they will make you pay for it. With more than your life."

She doesn't have to stress her point. I get it.

The door makes a loud clinking sound after she leaves. Alone with my thoughts, I look around the room.

There's no persistent smell of mold. The light that streams above the bed is warm and comforting, a little brighter than candlelight. I sit down on the bed and wrap my hands firmly around my knees.

Then I start to cry.

I cry for everything that I've seen.

I cry for everything that I went through.

I cry for all those women who are still in that dungeon of horrors.

But mostly, I cry for me.

The hot tears streaming down my face are tears of relief.

I'm not free, but I'm no longer there.

Back in that upstairs room, with all of its amenities and luxuries, I didn't know how good I had it.

M tried to warn me, but I didn't believe her. Who would? And then I learned about the true horrors of humanity. The true horrors of mankind.

I wipe one hot tear after another with the back of my sleeve, but more continue to flood. They come from the anger that's raging within me.

In the dungeon, I was lost.

Forgotten.

Death was my only relief. But something saved me.

I am reluctant to give credit to a higher power. Would a place like that exist in the first place if a higher power were anywhere near York?

No, it must be simpler than that.

There's going to be a competition. Someone here wants me to be a contestant. That's why I'm no longer in the dungeon.

I wipe my eyes again, and this time no more tears emerge. I lie down on my bed. My pillow is like a soft cocoon. I've been through hell, but the journey is not over yet. It's only the beginning.

Now, I know my place.

I am a prisoner.

A captive.

A slave.

I am without power.

But I have other things.

I have my head and my heart.

I will learn the rules of this place so that I can play my best hand.

It's my only hope of getting my freedom.

AS TIME PASSES, my physical wounds start to heal. In the small plastic mirror above the toilet, I see my black eye fading away. The bruises around my arms and legs first turn a sickly yellowish color then slightly green before disappearing entirely.

After a while, it's almost as if nothing happened.

Almost.

Here, food arrives three times a day and there are vegetables, pasta, and fish. Every few days, I even get some dessert. A slice of apple pie. A black and white cookie. An orange.

Here, no one comes to my cell besides the guards who bring the meals. At night, I still wake up with nightmares every few hours, terrified of what awaits me in the darkness.

Are they just waiting for me to get strong before sending someone to my cell? Will tonight be the night? But as days turn into weeks, even the nightmares start to subside.

Besides the guards, I don't have contact with anyone else. Occasionally, I peer through the plexiglass window of my door for a glimpse of the outside world. There are other doors just like mine leading to other cells.

Who is being kept there? How did they end up here?

Kept in isolation, you have a lot of time to think.

Mistakes you made.

Things you should or shouldn't have done.

All the steps you took that might have led to you being here.

I shouldn't have said. He did this because I insulted him.

I shouldn't have worn that. He did this because of how short my skirt was.

But why do I feel this insatiable need to blame myself?

Is it because I'm a woman or a victim?

Either way, it's crap. None of this was my fault. Not a single thing.

Someone who does something like what has been done to me is capable of evil. He's a sociopath, incapable of having empathy for another. No amount of clothing or makeup or lack thereof on my part made him that way.

* * *

TIME CONTINUES TO PASS, however slowly. I don't know how long I will be here, but I start to think of things to do to occupy myself. I need to get strong. Both in mind and body.

I've never been one to enjoy working out, but within the confines of this cell, it feels like a relief. I start slow. One day, I do ten lunges. The next, I do twenty. Then I add ten push-ups. I struggle through them, but within a few weeks, I can do fifty a day.

Soon, I spend at least an hour a day on physical activity. Running in place. Jumping jacks. Crunches. Stretches. And then yoga. It feels good to stretch my limbs every day and challenge my body.

In addition to working out my body, I start to work out my mind. I sit down at the table and pick up the pen. I begin small. I arrange words into sentences. Then sentences into paragraphs.

I don't want to write about this place, though. York is too dark and dreary.

I want to take my mind somewhere else.

At first, I struggle with even the simplest things. I stare at the blank page. Write a sentence. Cross it out. Write another. I don't know what to write; I just know that I have to write. But I persist.

Thoughts are swirling around in my mind and I need an outlet.

PART IV
A DIFFERENT KIND OF
PRISON

EASTON

DANCER IN THE DARK…

I hate York. I hate everything it stands for. I hate everyone here. They are greedy, possessive. Damaged.

But who am I kidding? I'm greedy, possessive, and damaged. I learned from the best, of course.

My father. The King of York.

Out in the real world, he is just the CEO of a Fortune 500 company. But here, on this island, he is the King. Whatever he says goes and you will be damned if you go against him.

As I wait for my name to be called, I hate myself for coming back here. Of course, I didn't have a choice.

I am the son of York. It doesn't matter that I am the youngest and the black sheep. He is having his biennial competition and everyone from the royal family, no matter how estranged, has to attend.

To understand my father, you have to understand insatiable desire.

For money.

For power.

For women.

For sin.

Nothing is ever enough and no *one* is ever enough. Well, there is one exception.

Abbott.

Abbott is my older brother and he is a carbon-copy of our father. Same ravenous desire to make his mark on the world. However painful and deep.

"Easton?" Mirabelle comes out with a clipboard.

She's in her fifties and has been my father's secretary ever since I was a baby. Mirabelle dresses modestly and always wears her hair in a French braid. She is pretty and kind and I have no idea how she has worked for such evil for so many years. Or what my father has on her to keep her in her position.

I follow her down the hallway toward my father's quarters in the house. The island is about ten miles across, and our residence is, of course, the largest place here. It's over 30,000 square feet and sits on over twenty acres. In addition to the main house, it also has a number of guesthouses on the property for visiting family guests and dignitaries. My father occupies about 10,000 square feet of the house with his private rooms.

Mirabelle knocks loudly before opening the last door at the end. His office. It hasn't changed since I was a toddler - the only one that isn't completely renovated every few years. This is the place where my father makes his real home.

When I walk in, I find him sitting behind a large oak desk relaxing with a book. The walls of the room are a library, lined with first editions.

But this isn't one of those show libraries that are popular with the wealthy class. My father has actually read all of these books.

My father doesn't look up from his book until I am standing squarely before him. I glance at the cover. It's the first English-language edition of Alexander Dumas' *The Count of Monte Cristo*.

My mind flashes back to the conversation we had on the eve of the first biennial competition.

"An ironic choice, don't you think?" I asked when I spotted him reading this very book.

"How so?" he asked in his usual arrogant tone.

"Well, you're about to have a competition to find

a new wife, forcing unjustly imprisoned women to fight for an opportunity to marry you. And here you are, sitting on the porch reading a book about a man who was unjustly imprisoned."

My father looked up at me with scorn in his eyes. I've never talked to him like that before, but I'd just turned eighteen and was bursting with arrogance. And then I said something even more stupid.

"But then again, Count of Monte Cristo later escaped and got his revenge. Is that what you secretly hope one of your wives will do?" I stared deeply into his eyes.

"Perhaps, I'm making a mistake," he said after a moment. I waited for him to continue.

"It doesn't seem to me like you are quite ready to go off to that Ivy League college of yours this fall given how little you seem to know."

And with that, he sentenced me to a year of hard labor on his remote ranch among the rocks of Nevada. 365 days of living in a small cell, sleeping five hours a night, working twelve hours a day, getting beatings every two days regardless of whether I followed the rules or not.

The other men there were others who'd stood up to the King of York. Some had been whistleblowers at his companies. Others had said something off-color about him to the press. All had disappeared suddenly in the middle of the night, never to be heard from again.

The guards were all chosen for the job because they had a cruelty streak and liked to see people in pain. They knew who I was and they were authorized to do with me as they pleased.

Exactly one year later, a Learjet came for me to take me back home to York and the guards were scattered among my father's other camps. Only they weren't guards anymore. They were prisoners. Their crime? Putting their hands on the Prince of York.

My father closes his book on his lap and says, "It's nice to see you again, Easton."

EASTON

THE MEETING...

He looks me up and down, taking note of every imperfection. I am used to his analysis. His scrutiny. We have not seen each other in a year. I only come here for the functions that I absolutely cannot miss. The rest of the time I stay away. But it's surprising how small the world is when your father is the King of York.

"You look well," he says.

"As do you, sir."

I've called him sir since I was a child.

I stand before him with hands by my sides. I am dressed in a tailored suit from Savilee Row in London. It is hot and humid outside, but in this room, we might as well be on his family estate in Scotland.

Dark wood and gloom are streaming in through the windows. I look through the one to his left.

Bald landscape. Gray skies. It's the northern Highlands, the place we often frequented when I was a kid. When mom was still alive.

The scene outside the windows isn't real, of course. At least, not here. Nothing but a video being streamed in from halfway around the world. I look back at my father. He must be feeling nostalgic.

"Scotland, huh?" I ask.

We both look out of the window and watch a black bird fly by. I wonder what's going on outside of this projected reality. Bananas hanging on the trees. Bugs buzzing around. The drizzle of the tropical afternoon rain bouncing against the glass.

"We should go back there together sometime," he announces. "You loved it as a child."

I'm taken aback a little by the statement. My father isn't one for expressing his emotions and this is probably the nicest thing he's said to me in years.

"Yes, I did enjoy it," I agree. Neither of us says anything for a few moments.

"How long are you staying?"

I shrug. "Through the month, of course."

"I figured. And after?"

"I have to get back to work," I say.

He looks away, displeased.

"I could barely get this month off. They don't really look upon a month long vacation too kindly on Wall Street."

He frowns again.

"Why do you work there? Is it just to annoy me?"

There are some perks to it, I want to say.

"Of course not."

"You can have an upper management position at any of the companies that I own. You know that."

"I want to make a name for myself," I say with a shrug.

"Even if you never take a penny from me and make your whole fortune yourself, they'll never give you credit for it. You'll always be my son."

Unfortunately, he's right. I sigh.

"Easton, you are smart. Cunning. But you know that already." My father continues his lecture. "You're smarter than Abbott. Don't tell him that, of course. Yet, here you are, wasting your time working in some lowly associate position at some investment bank."

"You own an investment bank," I point out.

"Eh." He waves his hand. "I want you to take over for me someday. Not one investment bank. But my whole...empire. How are you going to do that if you don't have any experience running my business?"

I stare at him. I've never heard him say this before. I never knew that I was even in the competition.

"Don't look at me like that."

"I'm just surprised, that's all. I thought that Abbott—"

"Abbott is a hot head," my father says, standing up from behind the desk. "He likes women too much. He has his indiscretions. I can't leave my empire to him."

I shake my head. This is news to me.

"So, what do you say?" he asks after a moment.

I shake my head. "What are you asking exactly?"

"I'm asking you to stay here. To learn the ropes. I want you to get educated about how we do things."

I shake my head and look away. No, I know how they do things. And I want no part of it.

"I know that you think me finding a new wife every two years is...cruel. But the thing is that I get bored. None of them ever live up to...your mother."

That's because she was never your slave, I want to say, but I bite my tongue. Just because he's talking to me so openly right now, doesn't mean he isn't capable of flipping like a switch.

"They don't act like it, but they all want to be here. You know that," my father says.

"I don't think so," I mumble.

"Please." He waves his hand. "They're women. And a woman wants nothing more in life than to be the most powerful woman around."

"Wouldn't that apply to men as well?" I ask with a tinge of sarcasm.

"It's just a game, son. You know that. If they really don't want to marry me, they don't have to. But the ones that make it to the final round, they are begging for the life that I'm offering them. They have gotten a taste of the power and wrath that I have and they crave it."

There is no use in arguing with him on this. It's his position and it's what helps him sleep at night.

"So, how about this? Stay, just for another month after, and I'll show you how we run things. Who knows, you might like it. Some things are for sure. You won't have to clock in seventy-hour weeks for that paltry salary of yours."

There it is. The smugness. The hatred. My father has contempt for anyone who is poorer than him and just about everything in America, let alone the world, is poorer than he is.

"I make $150,000 a year."

"Really? That's it? Who can live on that? I spend more than that on scotch in two months."

"Well, you do drink a lot of scotch."

He starts to laugh. A low bellowing thunder emanates deep from his stomach. I can't help but smile.

"I CAN'T," I say definitively. "Not this time. I'll lose my job."

Annoyed, my father spins around and stares into the distance. He has cut me off completely and isn't giving me a cent toward any of my expenses. Not even to pay back my school loans, which stand at about $140,000. I follow his lead and stare out the window. The rain falls straight down in sheets and Scotland has never looked more dreary, cold, and welcoming.

EASTON

WHEN I GO TO SEE MY BROTHER...

The meeting with my father goes as well as can be expected. I'm proud of myself for not giving in. I'm even prouder of myself for keeping my mouth shut and not telling him exactly what I think about him. Ever since that year in Nevada, I learned to fight battles with him in my own way. He thinks he's winning, but I'm just waiting. Someday, it will be my turn.

I have not seen Abbott yet, but I have heard the gossip. The guards talk a lot when they think no one is listening. And they should know better, someone is always listening. Mirabelle fills me in on some of the details as well, however, discreetly and tactfully.

I nod and listen to her version and see it all too clearly. I am not under any misapprehension about what my brother is capable of. When I was fifteen, I hacked into the security system from my computer and saw what he and three of his friends did to the girls in the dungeon. He was only twenty-one, but he was ruthless.

Before that day, I'd looked up to Abbott. He was my older brother. Someone who taught me how to play baseball and ride a bike. He was there for me after our mother died, in ways that our father never was. But after that day, I see him only as a monster. A monster I have to play nice with.

"I see that you've been up to your old tricks," I say, walking into his quarters on the other side of the house.

It's technically an apartment since it's connected to the main house, but it has five-bedrooms, four bathrooms, a den, and a 1,000 square foot kitchen with its own staff.

Abbots is sitting in the living room, in front of a 100-inch television, playing video games. The bruises on his face are just starting to heal.

"This is nothing," he says, without looking away from the screen. "The guards are just a bunch of gossip girls."

I grab a beer from the fridge and sit down next to him.

"You look good," he says, taking a brief pause from the game.

"As well as can be expected." I shrug.

"How's that job of yours going?" he asks, as if working for a living is the funniest thing in the world. "You get sick of it yet?"

"Not sick enough to come back here," I say.

"Oh, please, what's so bad about being here? Just a bit of fucking around. A lot of fucking. Some hunting. Maybe a surfing session or two. And then sitting in on board of trustees meetings once or twice a month. You know, you could do a lot worse."

I shrug.

"I don't want to depend on Father for everything."

Abbott rolls his eyes. "He's not that bad," he adds.

"Am I hearing you right?" I ask. "Aren't you the same kid who got sent away for six months to Arizona?"

"You mean camp?" Abbott asks nonchalantly.

Camp is what Father calls our periods of imprisonment and abuse.

"And then, didn't he send you away to Maine for another nine months when you were twenty-three?"

I ask. "Don't you think that twenty-three is a little too old for...camp?"

I don't know the precise details of what happened there, but from what I heard, it was somewhere between what I went through in Nevada and what the women are going through down below.

"Let bygones be bygones." Abbott waves his hand. "You know what your problem is, little brother? You never let things go."

I shake my head.

"And you know what your problem is?" I ask. "You will forgive anyone anything if they set you up with a few hundred billions. Well, guess what? It's just money, Abbott. It's just fucking money."

"Don't you get it? After all this time, don't you finally get it?" Abbott asks.

"Get what?" I ask.

He puts down his controller and turns to me. He leans forward a few inches and whispers, "Money is everything."

I RETURN to my room with a heavy heart. This is going to be one long month. And, on top of that, I am going to have to work a ton of overtime when I return to New York just to have the luxury of spending all these days off here.

Fuck!

I grab my swimming trunks and head to the only place around here that gives me any peace.
The ocean.

The sand is as white as snow. Digging my toes into it, it reminds me of powdered sugar - cool, soft, and extremely fine. I glide into the turquoise water. The air is warm, but the water is warmer. It's shallow for miles and warms up quickly in the tropical air. As I lie on my back with the sun kissing my face, I wonder how such a beautiful place can be so dark and ugly.

How can such horror exist here?

Of course, I know how. Everyone does.

York isn't like anywhere else.

Nothing about what goes on here is a secret, at least not from the rich and powerful. Most of the prominent heads of state know about this place and visit it frequently.

You would be surprised to learn just how many democratically elected leaders of enlightened countries have a taste for the illicit. I'm not even talking about the dictators and the unapologetic fascists who want nothing more than to see the powerless humiliated.

But besides heads of state, there are the leaders of other powerful organizations. The director of the FBI. The CIA. Secretary of State. They've all been here. They've all been to our parties and they've all enjoyed York's twisted delights.

This place is my father's dream come true. A secret island far away from civilization where men with lots of zeros in their bank accounts and very little moral fiber can do as they will. For him, it is not enough to simply rule a company and be a billionaire many times over.

He craves more.

More power.

More wealth.

More influence.

So, he bought this island and named himself the King.

At first, it was just a joke. *Haha, Mr. York is King. King of York. How charming.*

What is the only thing that a billionaire wants? To be King, of course.

But after a few years, it suddenly became reality. Away from America and the prying eyes of the world, all of his powerful friends - CEOs, CFOs,

Captains, Directors, Secretaries, Generals, Prime Ministers, and Presidents, started to refer to him as the King of York.

Imagine that, the Vice President of the United States calling the CEO of a Fortune 500 company and in a faint whisper referring to him as 'your majesty.'

The thing about York is that it's unlike anywhere else in the world. It's not only a kingdom; it's a secret kingdom. No one really knows about it because everyone knows about it.

On paper, there is no kingdom of York. This is just a private island owned by a very wealthy man who likes to throw lavish parties for his friends. But what wealthy man doesn't?

What I am sure that all of his powerful friends do not know, however, is that there is no such thing as a secret on the island of York. They come here to indulge in their desires, to do bad things because everyone does bad things. They feel safe and protected. And they are. Until my father needs something. Then they will find out the truth about this place. There is no privacy here. Everything is recorded and all of those recordings are saved on servers far away from here. And those men- because, who are we kidding, they are mostly men after all -

those men, will do anything to keep their secrets. And I mean, anything.

So, why don't I stand up to my father?

Why don't I fight for what's right?

Why don't I stand up to evil when I know that it's committed every day both in the dungeons of York and in its lavish quarters?

There's no point. How can one man stand up to all that? How can he possibly win?

"Hey!" Abbott runs over to the edge of the water and waves to me. I swim closer to shore.

"I got the tape of what that little bitch did to me!" he says, holding his phone. "Want to see it?"

EASTON

WHEN I SEE HER...

*A*bbott gets some sort of sick pleasure from watching himself be beat up. Normally, people would be appalled by what he did to make a woman act that way, but he's turned on.

"No, I don't really want to see it," I say, diving back under a wave.

"Oh, c'mon! You have to."

I walk out of the water and let myself air dry in the soft sun. He holds the phone up to my face. I glance down. It's a recording from her room. The image is crystal clear and I can hear every word.

"Why am I watching this again?" I ask.

"She surprised me," he says. "She doesn't look like the type to put up a fight. Frankly, I thought that

128

she would just lie there and close her eyes or something lame like that."

"You're an asshole." I shake my head. "You know that rape is illegal in all countries in this world, right?"

"Well, it's a good thing that I live in York, right? And I'm the Prince of York."

"How long are you just going to lie there on the bed like that?" I ask. "And why are your boots so dirty?"

"I'd just gone hunting earlier. And you know how killing something always makes me horny."

I want to roll my eyes, but I restrain myself.

Suddenly, I see her. She comes out of the bathroom and stares at him. Her face twists with fear. But there's something else. There's something about her that's so... familiar.

Oh my God. Of course.

It's her.

She's the woman I met at the charity event in Philadelphia.

I was sure that she got out. But how? How is she here? I warned her. I saw her take another cab.

"You enjoying this?" Abbott asks, licking his lips.

"You mean, you getting the shit beat out of you by a little girl? Yes, actually, I am."

"Hey, I'll be the first to admit that she caught me off guard. But I'll get mine, you'll see."

"What do you mean?"

"I have some plans for her. A bit of revenge."

I'm taken aback by that. Normally, anyone who raises their hands to the Prince, let alone hits him with a chair and gives him a concussion, is sent to the dungeons.

"Are you going to see her down there?" I ask.

He's not supposed to go there, but Abbott isn't one for rules. Besides, we both know that there are laws that our father enforces and others that he just looks the other way on.

"No, not this time."

I stare at him blankly.

"I begged for mercy for her," Abbott says with a mischievous twinkle in his eyes. I stare at him, dumbfounded.

"What are you talking about?" I ask. "Everyone knows that once someone is sent to the dungeons, they are not getting out. Ever."

"Well, Father made an exception."

"Why?"

"To shake things up? Frankly, I have no idea. I was shocked when I heard, but happy, too. But I guess he took a liking to her. 'Cause he has put her back into the competition."

Back into the competition? The words just stay there in mid-air suspended between us, as if we are in a comic strip.

"Don't look so shocked," Abbott says.

"How can I not be? This is unprecedented."

"Well, everything is, until it happens, right?" Abbott says nonchalantly.

"It just seems so...unwise."

"You think she should go back?"

"No, of course not," I say.

And I don't. Not at all. When I first heard about the dungeons through whispers from the guards, I begged my father to put an end to it. What did he do? He denied their existence. But, of course, they exist. I have seen the video recordings. And not just of the one Abbott has had a starring role in.

"What do you think made him change his mind?" I ask. "I mean, what happened to her down there?"

"Oh, finally! You're coming around from your good guy ways!" Abbott exclaims. "I'll send you the video."

"No, no, that's not what I mean," I start to say, but it's too late.

Abbott picks up his phone and logs into his cloud account. The shirt that I threw on the sand along with the rest of my clothes vibrates. The video has arrived to my inbox.

"You aren't supposed to have this," I say. Another one of Father's strict orders. No one is supposed to watch the recordings of what's going on there.

"What else is new?" Abbott shrugs. "Honestly, the rules of this place. You know, it can be quite stifling here if you follow all of them."

"Yes, I know." I nod.

"You see, that's your problem, Easton. You're too law-abiding. I mean, you are a Prince of York. Act like it once in a while. Father will respect you more."

"The last thing I need is that asshole's respect," I whisper under my breath. We're outside, on the beach, far away from the house, and yet I'm still not sure if a recording of this conversation will get back to him.

"I know you think he's a dick. So do I," Abbott says. "But he's not as mean as he used to be. He has softened up a lot."

"Yeah, right," I say.

"Yes. Right," he confirms. "I'm not sure if it's his old age or what, but he's a lot nicer now. Always talking about his legacy and shit like that."

I shrug and look out at the horizon. The sun is dropping into the ocean, painting the sky in gold and peach. I yearn to be out there, somewhere in the distance, away from the madness of this place.

"You should visit more often, Easton. If you did, you'd notice that he's not the same."

I shrug again. I can't trust Abbott. He's my brother, but he's always playing a game. When Abbott plays games, he plays to win.

"Isn't he holding the competition again?" I finally ask. Abbott nods.

"Well, having women compete for your hand in marriage, against their will, doesn't sound like much of a change for me."

"It's not a big deal anymore, Easton. I mean, he doesn't really take it that seriously anymore. Besides, most of them are really into it."

"Are you listening to yourself, Abbott? Most of them? Shouldn't all of them be into it? And, at the end, do they still have to marry him and have his children?"

Abbott glares at me.

"You know what your problem is? You're too judgmental."

A low bellowing laugh builds somewhere in the

bottom of my stomach and spreads throughout my whole body.

"What happens to the women who don't proceed through the rounds?" I ask. I know the answer, of course, but I want to hear it from Abbott.

"They don't move on in the competition."

"And what does that mean exactly?"

"They are sold off."

"They are sold off at an auction," I specify. "To terrible men who do who knows what with them and to them."

"Life is a bitch, Easton. So what?"

"Yes, I know. I am very well aware of this fact."

"So, what do you want from me?"

I take a step closer to him and whisper, "What I want from you is to stop making excuses for that son of a bitch that we call our father."

I grab my clothes and collide into his shoulder as I walk past him. Surprisingly, he doesn't punch me or pull me down to the ground. He just takes a step back and lets me go.

"He's still our father!" Abbott yells after me.

I ignore him and instead watch as my feet sink deeper and deeper into the snow-white sand with each step.

"He's different now, Easton. You'll see. He would

never send you to Nevada now!" Abbott screams at the top of his lungs, barely in earshot.

He knows very well what happened to me in Nevada. Our father had his men show him the videos. They also showed them to me. A number of times. They were meant to serve as a reminder of what I'd done and what happens to those who stand up to him. Well, I received the message loud and clear. And nothing is ever going to change my mind about him. Ever.

When I get back to my apartment on the far end of the house, I stomp my feet to knock off some of the sand and plop onto the bed.

The first round of competition is tomorrow. Everyone, who is anyone in York, will be there. The most important of us will be required to participate. I need to rest so that my contempt and anger doesn't show on my face. Yet, my mind keeps drifting back to one thing: the video that Abbott sent me.

He's not supposed to have it and neither of us are supposed to see it. But, of course, Abbott has his ways. He has managed to survive in this house for a lot more years than I have without igniting my father's wrath. Yes, he definitely has some resources at his disposal.

I thumb the screen of my phone trying to decide

what to do. I know I shouldn't watch it. Not because my father has forbidden it, but because I don't want to see anything that happens. I jump into the shower to wash off the salt and sand. My mind races as I lather my hair and body.

What happened down there?

What did she do that made her stand out?

What is it about her that changed my father's mind?

With soap still running down my face, I get out of the shower. Wiping my hands with a towel, I grab my phone and log in.

EASTON

WHEN I WATCH THE VIDEO...

*T*he screams are deafening.

I turn down the volume. I can't bear to hear them.

The dungeon is dark, but the lighting is sufficient. It's like a terrible movie from which you can't look away. But there isn't anything amateurish about it.

Someone has edited this video. There are cuts. Multiple angles. Zoom in. Zoom out. Someone watched this video a number of times to get just the right angles. Did Abbott do this?

The only thing that's missing is a soundtrack.

What kind of music would enhance the experience of a torture chamber? Something German? Classical? Perhaps, a virtuoso pianist.

I see the fear in her eyes. Tears are glistening on her cheeks. One tear runs down the outside of her face, pausing slightly in hesitation.

I cannot see the men's faces. They crowd around her like animals after a kill. She is chained to the wall.

Restrained.

Helpless.

She screams and begs just like the rest of them do. I cannot bear to watch the rest. I fast-forward. It goes on for hours and hours.

Different days. Different men.

Same dungeon. Same horror. Same screams.

And then it stops.

Just like that.

In the middle of the video, the woman transforms into someone else before my eyes. She does not beg anymore. She does not fight. There's a far away look on her face. Glazed eyes. Lost in some other world.

She is there, but she's not there.

Her body remains with them. But her mind flies away.

They yell at her to come back. Shake her. Slap her. But she does not return.

She is not drunk or high. It's almost as if she has

transported herself to some other place, on another plane of existence.

The men keep coming. The cruelty continues, but she is no longer the same. I have no doubts that she still feels pain. Of course, she does. Yet, she finds some peace.

I turn off my phone.

So, that's why my father caved. Abbott had shown him the video and he just couldn't resist having a woman like that in his competition.

Which wife is this again? The competition runs every two years, so this must be the sixth.

Four of those have produced heirs. Most more than one. All except two are boys. This island is crawling with children of York.

It's not the kids' fault. Of course not. Who asks to be born into this world? Let alone into the kingdom of York?

For now, none of them can challenge Abbott as the one true heir to the throne. But what does the future hold? Many kingdoms have fallen apart over the hate that is bred into the children.

I have no intention of inheriting anything. Abbott knows that. He knows that as soon as our father moves on from this world to torment others in another world, he can take the throne. If he wants it. I know that he does.

I run my finger over the outline of my phone.

Who are you, Everly March? I do not dare to say her name out loud.

Undressed and shy, I remember the way she stood quietly in the corner. I was drawn to her even then. Is it her cold glare? Or her hot temper? Back then, she didn't know what she was capable of yet.

I tried to warn her. But it didn't work. Maybe I wasn't convincing enough.

Unfortunately, her only way out now is to win. I don't know exactly what happens to the other girls, but it's not good. Everyone has a debt to pay for knowing about this place.

What will this place do to you, Everly March?

Will it force you to rise to the occasion? Will you fight with all of your might, or will you give in?

Will you do anything to live? Or will you let them take your life from you?

Will you become my new stepmother, even though you are younger than I am? Two of my other ones are also.

Or will you be sold off to the wolves?

Will you bear my father's children, my future

brothers and sisters? Or will you spend the rest of your life in a foreign land?

No matter what, you will spend the rest of your life in chains.

We all do, because this is York. York is where darkness lives.

I dread this day, but as with all dreaded days, it comes anyway. As the sun starts to set, the first round of competition begins. It's not fair, just like everything else about this contest. None of the women know that they are being judged.

The audience get their seats behind a large screen in my father's private screening room. Only his top advisors and friends gather here. Everyone else meets in the theater at the other side of the house.

I wish I could sit back in the dark and watch with the rest of them. But, unfortunately, I have to participate.

As always, Ferguson Groff helps me get ready. He is an English butler with a knack for discretion and he has been my servant since I was a child. He's in his early sixties, and he's the only person I really miss when I'm not here. Ferguson is not one for emotion, but when he greets me this afternoon, I notice that his eyes look a little damp.

"It's so great to see you, Ferguson," I say, giving him a warm hug.

"You are looking well, Mr. York."

As a son of York, my official title here is Mr. York or Prince of York. I've considered changing it, going by something else back home. But there is very little distinction between this place and the real world, so my father is bound to find out about it.

"Are you ready for the competition?" Ferguson asks tactfully. He knows better than to ask me if I'm excited for it.

"As ready as I will ever be, I guess," I say with a shrug.

Ferguson shows me the suits that he has picked out for me and I point to the first one there. I trust his judgement and the last thing I want to do is to give this whole affair any more thought than I should. As long as it's appropriate attire, I'm fine with it.

* * *

THE FIRST ROUND is nothing more than a cocktail hour. That's it. There is no host yet. No announcer. Just a tastefully designed hall with tall cocktail tables and two bars at opposite ends. And the cameras, of course.

The purpose of the first round is to evaluate the women on their poise. The judges are seated in another room, and their job is to watch and listen to every word. They are interpreters. What does doing this or that say about this woman? What does that say about the other one?

They may be judges, but their influence is rather paltry. They assign scores, based on each contestant's performance and make suggestions. The final decision about everything is up to my father. It is his future queen after all.

I am escorted to the head of the line, right behind Abbott, and we walk into the room first. The rest of the men follow. I've met some of them. Others are here for the first time. It's a mixed bag of positions, ages, and looks.

The older ones are dignitaries and other high ranking men from around the world.

The younger ones are mainly bait. They have chiseled jawlines, beautiful eyes, and bodies of

Greek Gods. Some are online celebrities; others are legit movie stars.

The men don't know this, but they were invited to test the contestants.

Will they be drawn in by their beauty and charms? Or will they give the older ones a chance? And what exactly will they say to them? How will they act? Will they spend the night with them? And what exactly will they do?

Sleeping with someone isn't an immediate disqualification.

The woman who became queen six years ago, took a different man to her chambers every night. Sometimes, more than one. Sometimes, she even invited one of the other contestants to join them.

That year, my father was in the mood for someone who was ravenous and insatiable. There are no rules to this contest. I'd say it's rigged, but it would have to be rigged in someone's favor. And in this case, it's subject to nothing else but my father's whims.

Abbott and I get our drinks and position ourselves at the far end of the room. I don't want to be the first person any of the contestants talks to, and Abbott likes to get the feel for everyone in the competition before making his move. Typically, we don't know anything about any of the contestants.

Except this year, of course.

Except about Everly March.

After all the men are positioned around the room, the doors open again and the women enter. They are dressed in gowns. Most are long and sparkling, some are tight-fighting, and others are flowing. I don't know much about dresses, except that they all look beautiful.

I wonder about the excited expressions on their faces. Are they fake? An illusion to hide their true feelings. Or are they actually looking forward to this? The flawless airbrushed makeup and the wide smiles make it hard to tell.

I lean against the wall. As Prince of York, I have to mingle. Participate. But the degree of my involvement isn't specified, so I hang back. I have no interest in getting to know these poor women. Their fates have been sealed long before they arrived here.

I don't want to look for her.

I try not to.

But I can't help it.

Everly is one of the last ones to enter. Her long red gown sparkles as she walks. She's not an expert in wearing heels and it shows. She doesn't glide like some of the models here, but she doesn't stumble either. She's cautious and careful. She's the only one who is aware of the full darkness of this place.

Her dark hair is pinned around her temples with a delicate hair clip, bringing out her eyes. Instead of heading straight to the men, as most of the others do, she takes her time at the bar. Orders a drink, sits down on a stool, and faces away from the room.

I glance over at Abbott.

Something is bubbling up within him.

Is it anger? Desire? A bit of both?

He makes a move forward, but I grab his arm.

"You can't talk to her now," I say.

"Why not?"

"We're supposed to mingle. They're supposed to make their way around the room. If you go straight to her, you'll make a scene."

"So? Isn't that what we're doing here? Putting on a show?"

"You need to give her space," I insist.

I have no reason to hold him back, except that I want the judges to see her for who she is first. Before she does...frankly, I have no idea what she is going to do when she sees him, but whatever it is, it will likely get her disqualified.

"Fine," Abbott says, pushing me away. "I'm going to talk to that one instead."

Tall, blonde, and gorgeous. She's the quintessential example of Abbott's type.

I don't believe him. But much to my surprise, he does exactly that. He walks up to the blonde and offers to buy her a drink. Then he leads her to the other bar, clear across the room from Everly.

"Well, hello there." Someone comes up to me, running her fingers down my arm. She has dark piercing eyes and almond hair, so shiny it might be made of silk. She takes a sip of her drink and looks up at me with a mischievous smile.

"I'm number eleven," she says, extending her hand.

"Easton," I say, shaking her hand.

"It's very nice to meet you, Easton."

"So, how do you like it here?" I ask after a few moments of silence. I want her to go away, but she's persistent.

"It's beautiful. The white sand. The crystal blue waters. Really reminds me of home."

"Home?"

"I grew up on the Gulf coast of Florida. Near Sanibel."

I nod.

"Sounds nice," I mumble.

My eyes drift across the crowd.

Shit.

"Can you excuse me please?" I mumble and rush toward them.

EASTON

WHEN HE CAN'T HELP HIMSELF...

My brother just can't resist.

He craves conflict.

Loves it.

Lives on it.

It fuels every cell in his body. He's inching closer and closer to Everly.

She's still sitting at the bar turned away from me. Her blood red gown sweeps across the floor.

"Abbott!" I whisper loudly. "Abbott!"

He doesn't turn around. Once his mind is set on something, he remains steadfast in pursuing it.

What does he want with her? Does he want to confront her? To threaten her?

I don't really know. Is this why he pled for her release?

I watch as he leans on her, draping his arm around her shoulder. Her brushes her hair from her neck. Her shoulders go up a little, in surprise.

She looks up at him.

Maybe I've made a mistake. Perhaps, it's not her. But as soon as she swivels around, I know that I haven't.

Everly tilts her face. Her eyes open widely and she looks at him inquisitively.

"Hello, stranger," she says without balking at his touch. Her lips, the color of the dying sun, open slowly and form a smile.

Stopping a few feet away, I'm just within earshot. I don't interrupt.

"I didn't think you would be happy to see me," Abbott says.

Without removing his arm from her bare shoulder, he nods to the bartender, asking for a refill.

"And why is that?" she asks.

"Well, you remember? We didn't start off on the best of terms."

"I've gotten a lot wiser since then," she says. "And you...you've gotten a lot better looking."

Abbott laughs.

"A shower and a tuxedo go a long way with me," she adds, taking a sip of her drink.

I shouldn't be here, but I can't pull myself away.

Who is this woman?

She looks like Everly from the outside. An upscale, dressed up version of her, anyway. But the shy unsure girl I met at the Oakmont is all but gone. It's as if she has aged two decades in the time she has been here, without getting one single crease on her face.

"Nineteen, I'd like for you to meet my brother," Abbott says loudly. "Easton, why don't you stop spying from over there and come say hi?"

Her face falls as soon as she sees me, but she tries to catch herself.

"You're Abbott's brother?" she asks.

"Easton," I say, extending my hand. "It's nice to meet you."

Everly clenches her jaw and purses her lips. Her eyes throw daggers of hate at me. She recognizes me. She thinks that I'm the one responsible for her being here.

"Isn't this a beautiful island?" I ask.

She inhales deeply, about to say something mean, but then changes her mind and nods.

"Well, it's made only so much more beautiful by the women in this room," I say. "You being on top of that list, of course."

"Thank you," she hisses through her teeth.

These are blanket pleasantries. I'm not trying to be kind or sweet or to give her a compliment.

I'm just trying to keep her mouth shut about what I did at the Oakmont.

Why is it that she was able to play her role so expertly when she saw Abbott, but not when she saw me?

Lucky for both of us, Abbott doesn't seem to notice a thing. He is too enamored with her transformation to pay attention to anything else.

"Well, I'd love to stay and chat, but I have to make my rounds," Abbott says, taking Everly's hand. "But I'll see you later, I hope."

"Yes, definitely."

I wait for him to find his new mark and take off in her direction. Then I ask Everly to follow me out onto the balcony.

"Please?" I ask and place my hand on hers. She swivels the stool to face away from me. "The sky is beautiful now and we will have some privacy there."

Eventually, and with great reluctance, she agrees.

As I escort her to the balcony on the other side of the room, I try to put my hand on the small of her back, but she takes a few steps forward to get away from me.

The balcony isn't really a balcony in the normal sense. It comes in at almost two-thousand square feet and overlooks the translucent waves below.

I lead Everly to the far end, where we are a bit out of the way of the cameras and the sound is muffled by the wind coming off the water.

"We don't have much time," I whisper. "The camera people will be here soon."

"I don't need time," Everly says. "I have nothing to say to you."

"I'm sorry that you're here," I say in a hushed tone.

"Me, too. And I'm also sorry that I believed you and got into that cab."

"I had nothing to do with that. I tried to help you."

"Help me? You? You're the one who told me not to trust my date," she whispers loudly.

"I thought that you would be safe getting into that cab alone."

"Whatever," Everly says, waving her hand. "I'm done with this place and these games you all play here."

"I'm not playing a game."

"Yes, you are. You're playing the role of the hero.

Pretending to help me, just to betray me at the very end."

I glance into the distance. The camera people are coming out onto the balcony.

"I want to help you," I whisper.

"You did," she whispers back. "You showed me how this game is played. I can't trust anyone in York. And I never will."

Cameras surround us, and Everly quickly takes my hand in hers.

"Thank you for saying those kind words to me," she says. "It was a pleasure to meet you."

PART V
FIRST ROUNDS

EVERLY

WHEN I AM SHOWN...

The blood red gown makes a quiet swishing sound as I walk.

The first two steps in my four-inch heels are unsteady, and I have to lean against the wall for support. The guards lead the way and eventually I manage to get a better handle on my footing and stop tripping. The guards, dressed in tuxedos, show me down a long hallway and through a doorway. There, in a poorly-lit room with extremely high ceilings, I join the rest of the women.

Some talk among themselves. Others stand motionless, staring into space.

Something is about to happen, but we don't know what.

I glance at the guards who surround us. Their

faces are flat and expressionless, revealing nothing of what is about to happen.

Then a spotlight comes on in the distance and a brunette in a form-fitting strapless canary-yellow gown walks onto the stage.

Suddenly, it hits me where we are.

Backstage.

All light around us seems to vanish and the audience outside gets quiet. I stand on my tiptoes to get a better view of what's going on out there.

The music comes on, a slow moving melody, and part of the stage starts to rotate. The woman begins to spin, showing her body from all angles.

Standing proudly with her shoulders back, she points her chin to the ceiling.

A man comes out, dressed in an elegant tuxedo which accentuates his large build. He runs his hand over her shoulders and up and down her neck. She tilts her head toward him, as if she is enjoying it.

Actually, maybe she is. I have no idea.

Suddenly, the man pulls out a knife from his breast pocket. I expect her eyes go grow wide with fear, but they don't. Instead, she gives him a wink, leans over, and licks the blade.

I guess Shakespeare was right, I say to myself. All the world's a stage and we are all players.

The man brings the knife to her chest. The point makes a little indentation in her breast as they rise and fall with each of her breaths.

He teases her with his knife.

One prick.

Then another.

Not at her skin but at the threads of her dress.

Five pricks later and the dress falls to the floor.

The stage starts to move faster, making them appear, as if they are waltzing.

The woman steps out of her dress and kicks it away.

She presses her lips to the man's and runs her hands down his body until she reaches his belt. Then she starts to undo it.

The audience explodes in applause as the man unclasps the woman's bra, freeing her breasts. The women backstage join in with the applause.

Reality melts away and morphs into the unknown.

I cannot distinguish between what is authentic and fake anymore.

A few moments later, the couple is waltzing naked with each other.

Their hands melt into one. Their legs intertwine. Her lips become his lips. When the song comes to an end, their rotating stage moves further away from the audience until the lights fall and they disappear.

"Wasn't that magnificent?" A long-legged, Amazonian beauty turns toward me.

"Yes, it was...something indeed," I mumble.

"You don't seem impressed."

"No, of course, I am," I say.

"Oh, okay, because you had me scared for a moment," she says.

She has a thick accent - Brazilian perhaps? She uses exaggerated hand gestures to get her point across and introduces herself as Alessandra.

"You're scared?" I ask. "Why?"

"Well, you know, I don't know what's going to happen when I go out there."

Suddenly, the reality hits me across the face like an open palm.

"So, that's not a show?" I ask. "She just did that...spontaneously?"

Alessandra nods and smiles broadly. "Exciting, isn't it?!"

Shivers run down my spine. I'm not one for theatrics, to say the least.

In school, my stomach would get into knots whenever I even had to raise my hand in class. And

I'd have a full-on anxiety attack if I had to make a presentation.

Someone taps me on my shoulder. "You're next," a guard in a blue and white tuxedo says. I glare at her.

"No, there must be some sort of mistake," I start to protest.

"No," she says, definitively.

"But...no..." I try again. "What about all those women ahead of me? I thought I had...more time."

The guard shakes her head and takes me by my elbow.

"No, please," I plead.

A sob is starting to form in the back of my throat. My fingertips get ice cold.

"It's a mistake. I'm not next. You don't even know my name."

"You're next, number nineteen," she whispers into my ear. "You have to go out there, Everly, or they will send you back down to the dungeons."

So, this is not a mistake. I can't feel my body. A loud muffling sound blares in between my ears.

"But...I don't know what to do," I say. "What am I supposed to do out there?"

"Just go out to the center of the stage until you

see the X, stand there, and be yourself. But do as they say."

"What does that mean?" I ask as she pushes me out past the side curtains.

Suddenly, the spotlight is on me.

It bathes me in harsh, hot light.

I walk out onto the stage.

The hall is quiet and my heels make a loud clinking sound with each step.

I feel everyone's eyes on me and take a few deep breaths.

When I get to the black X, I stop and turn to face the crowd.

A sea of faces is looking at me.

Who are you people?

Do you know what's going on here?

A disembodied voice announces me as number nineteen and the stage starts to turn.

I plant my feet firmly and spin along with it.

I consider putting one of my feet out in front of me and pushing my hips to the other side, like I've seen girls do online.

But what's the fucking point?

I don't want to be here and I definitely don't want to be on stage.

I continue to stand with my legs slightly apart and my shoulders slouching down, in an effort to disappear off the face of the planet. Unfortunately, it doesn't work.

I should stand up straight. I should try harder.

But aren't I supposed to be myself?

The real me has no desire to straighten her shoulders.

If they want to see the real me, then this is who I am.

No one claps or makes a sound. The silence is deafening.

"Take off your dress, number nineteen," the announcer says.

A loud gasp comes from stage right.

The crowd erupts in applause.

But I just shake my head.

"Take off your dress," the announcer says, and again I shake my head.

"Take off your dress, now." His voice is getting impatient.

I look down at my gown.

What is it to take it off? It's no big deal.

I've done much worse.

They've done much worse to me.

So, why can't I do this?

I look out in the crowd. Hundreds of faces are looking at me.

Do they know about the depths of hell that this place really is?

Do they think this is a game?

A show?

Why not? I thought it was only a few minutes ago.

I can take off my gown.

Of course, I can.

But I refuse.

In this auditorium full of people, I feel like maybe, just maybe, I have a chance.

Will this get me kicked out of the competition? I don't know.

One thing is for sure.

I will be myself. If only once in this shitty place.

"No," I say defiantly, shaking my head.

The men come from each side of the stage. Both are dressed in tuxedos with their hair slicked back. They walk purposefully toward me and jump on the rotating platform.

Then, without saying a word, they grab at me.

One unzips my dress and the other one pulls it down to the floor.

Their movements are choreographed. Practiced.

But they don't stop there. One unclasps my bra and the other pulls it off. Within a matter of seconds, I'm standing topless in front of a hall of excited eyes.

"Get the fuck off me," I say, kneeing one in the balls as hard as I can.

Caught off guard, he topples over in pain.

The second one comes for my throat, and I punch him in the jaw. Much to my surprise, the punch lands well and he trips over his feet.

Three other men quickly run out, surrounding me. Two of them grab my arms and hold them behind my back.

There's nowhere to go. No point in fighting. There never was much of a point, but it felt damn good to hurt them.

Too bad these men will do much worse to me.

The man standing in front of me rips off my panties. I'm ready for what's about to come. I close my eyes to get away from here.

"No," the announcer says. "Do not touch her."

We all look up surprised.

"Let her go," the announcer says.

"But she has to be punished," one of the guards starts to protest.

"No, on King's orders, you will not touch her," the announcer says and they let me go.

"Give her her clothes," the announcer says. They hand me my bra and dress and I immediately put them back on.

"Let's have a round of applause for number nineteen, ladies and gentlemen," the announcer says. "As you can see, she's quite a fighter."

I leave the stage to a standing ovation.

WHEN I MAKE A MISTAKE...

When I get backstage, everyone congratulates me on my performance.

"Wow, you were amazing."

"So strong."

"Weren't you scared?"

"I can't believe they took it that far!"

I nod and thank them for their kind words. My head is still spinning over what happened.

"Oh my God, nineteen, you were...amazing! What a performance!" Alessandra yells, wrapping her arms around me. "How did you know to do that?"

I shrug. She's holding a bottle of water and I ask her for a sip.

"I really don't know what I'm going to do up there," she says. "Do you think I should also fight back?"

"I don't know, maybe," I say. "But it could also turn on you. I mean, I fought before and…it wasn't the best decision."

She narrows her eyes, inquisitively. "What do you mean?"

"Well, you know, back in the cell. The locked hotel room." I take another sip. She looks even more perplexed than before. Then it hits me.

"Wait, do you not know?" I ask.

"Know what?"

"Weren't you kept in a room like I was?"

She shakes her head. "Kept in a room? What are you talking about?"

We both stare at each other for what feels like an hour. It's long enough for me to notice that she has a little imperfection on her right iris, which makes her look even more breathtaking.

"You were kept in a room?" she asks in a whisper.

I nod. The shivers on the back of my neck warn me against telling her anything more, but for some reason I can't keep it to myself.

"It was a really nice room, but it was a cell anyway. I was told that men were going to come and

I shouldn't fight them. Just let them do what they want with me. Well, I didn't listen."

"So, what happened?"

"I fought one off and hurt him pretty badly so they took me down to the dungeons. That's where they did really bad shit to me."

I can't bring myself to say the word rape or any of the other ones that would describe what really happened.

Alessandra shakes her head and starts to laugh.

"Wow, you're good," she says, shaking her head. A big wide smile forms on her face.

I don't understand what she means.

"You're already competing. I thought that we could be friends, but you're just trying to scare me."

"I'm not," I whisper. "It really happened."

"C'mon, you expect me to believe that? That this place has some dungeons or men who come to your room and rape you? That's stupid."

"Why?"

"Because this is York. We are here to meet a desirable bachelor and to compete for his heart. That's all. It's a reality show that's not aired on television."

I shake my head.

"They would never do anything bad to us. We can come and go as we want."

"Please, you have to believe me," I plead. "This place isn't what you think it is."

But it's too late.

"I thought we could be friends. But I'm not going to be friends with someone who says these things," she says, waving her hand.

Then she turns on her heels and walks away from me.

Just as I'm about to follow her, an older woman with a tight bun and a severe expression on her face approaches. She's holding a clipboard in one hand and a pen in the other.

"You should not have done that, Everly," she says under her breath.

"Done what?" I play innocent.

"You are not to tell anyone in this contest what you have gone through, do you understand?"

I shrug.

"I thought that would be obvious, but I guess it requires saying. Unfortunately, your friend now knows too much."

"What does that mean?" I gasp.

"You are responsible for her elimination, Everly," the woman says.

Two men in tuxedos approach Alessandra and escort her to the stage. Her eyes light up and she practically jumps up in excitement.

It takes all of my effort to not follow her out there and tell her to run. But it's futile. Whatever is going to happen is going to happen regardless of what I do.

As soon as she is positioned on the rotating stage, the announcer begins.

"This is Alessandra Costa," he says. "She is 5'11 and 119 pounds. Her mother had nine children and she is the second youngest. The only girl."

Something is different about this. Details are disclosed. What are they doing?

My heart jumps into my chest. But Alessandra simply spreads open her shoulders and readjusts her hands on her waist. She is proud to be here. Like a beauty queen, she enjoys being judged.

"Alessandra has a college degree in early childhood education and she loves children. Let's begin the bidding."

The bidding?

The friendly expression on her face vanishes. Instead, confusion settles in on the ridge of her nose.

She is not expecting an auction.

Neither am I.

I look around the room.

The woman with the clipboard is standing very close to me.

Watching me.

She's making sure that I don't say another word.

The rest of the contestants look mesmerized, but interested more than confused.

"Alessandra, you are going to be progressing through the competition quite swiftly," the announcer says. "You are the lucky one to be auctioned off first."

The unsure expression on her face vanishes.

A smile appears.

"That's a good girl," the announcer goads her. "Now, why don't you give us a twirl?"

She's about to be sold off.

But to whom? I have no idea. No one good, that's for sure.

"I will start the bidding at one-hundred thousand dollars," the announcer says.

Alessandra's eyes light up, as if she's the one who will be getting the money.

I may not know much about this place, but we are not here to make money.

We are here to be used by people with money.

I'm certain that she will not be getting a penny from that use.

The numbers quickly climb.

$150,000

$235,000

$345,000

$505,000

$550,000

"Sold for five hundred and fifty thousand dollars," the announcer says proudly. Alessandra is so happy she can barely contain herself enough to step off the rotating portion.

When she gets backstage, she runs straight into my arms.

"Can you believe it? I'm going to get more than half a million dollars!" she exclaims.

"Alessandra," I start to say, but the woman next to me pinches my back. I glance back at her.

"Congratulations," she says to Alessandra. "You are our first winner."

WHEN I MOVE ON…

irst winner my ass, I want to say.

I want to say many things.

I want to tell Alessandra that she's not getting any of that money.

That she has just been sold into slavery.

That she will never see her family again.

That this is a house of horrors.

But she looks so happy.

Overjoyed.

I can't bring myself to do it. She will learn these things soon enough.

Will knowing them an hour earlier do anything but give her just an hour more of hurt and pain? Of course not.

"What's going to happen to her?" I hiss at the woman with the clipboard.

How can she be so callous? So uncaring about this? What made her this way? I wonder.

"A sultan bought her," she says. "So, I imagine she is going to live a long life as his new girlfriend. As long as he doesn't get bored with her."

I shake my head.

"Why...why am I here?"

"Someone wants you here."

"That's not a good answer."

"It's the only one I have."

I pace back and forth. Women in gowns start to glare back at me as they wait for their turn on r stage. They are just as eager as Alessandra was.

They congratulate her on her bid, as if she's the one who is pocketing the money.

They can't wait for their turn.

Are these women mad? Or am I?

Suddenly, I can't contain myself any longer.

"I have to talk to you," I say, running up to Alessandra and pulling her away into a dark corner.

What happened to waiting? For letting her figure it out on her own? I don't know.

Could you watch a car crash happen and not try

to do something, however futile and pointless? I thought I could.

"Get away from me!" she yells and pushes me back.

Just then, someone grabs my elbow and pinches it really hard. I wince in pain. Someone else pins my arm behind my back.

My shoulder blades throb and I can't break free.

"The Prince may want his revenge," the woman with the clipboard hisses in my ear, "but the King will only put up with so much disobedience."

I turn my face away from hers. She grabs my chin and forces it back.

Then she takes her hand and with an open palm slaps me clear across my face.

My cheek stings in pain.

Hot tears roll down my face.

I'm not entirely sure if my cheeks are burning from the pain or from the humiliation. I do everything in my power to stop more tears from coming, but it's all to no avail.

One sob turns into another and another.

"Shut up," the woman hisses and slaps me again.

And again.

I continue to cry as the guards pull me further into the recesses of the backstage area. We disappear into the darkness and none of the contestants seem to notice.

Behind the curtains, the woman with the clipboard tries to reason with me.

Her tone softens and she tells the guards to leave us alone.

Much to my surprise, they do as she says.

"You can't behave like this," she says. "You have to calm down. You have to play the game. You ended up in the dungeons, but you came back. You are the only one to ever come back, Everly."

She says my name. My real name.

"Do you understand that?" she asks.

I shrug.

"Is that a big deal?"

"You remember the dungeons, Everly?" she asks.

I nod.

"Do you want to go back?"

I shake my head.

"Then you don't want to test his patience."

"Whose?"

"Whoever is looking out for you. He pleaded for your mercy. He got you out of that dungeon. You don't want him to regret that decision."

I shrug.

"Do you not care what happens to you?" she asks, shaking my shoulders.

I look into her eyes.

Who am I kidding? Whatever is happening here is one hundred times better than what was happening there. I can't argue with that.

"Yes, I do," I say after a moment. "Of course, I do."

"Then make them want you."

I stare at her.

"Your performance out there intrigued them. But you need to continue. You need to surprise them. They are always watching."

"Who?"

"The judges," she says.

"So, what should I do?"

"For one, do not tell any of the other contestants about what you have been through. I don't know if any of them have been in the same place you have, but none of them have been to the dungeons. Assume they all want to be here. Like Alessandra did."

"But she's going to be hurt."

The woman shakes her head and looks away. "Of course, she will. You all will. You just made it that much worse."

"What?" I gasp.

"This was just a showing. This isn't even the first round. And because of what you said, they had to have an auction to sell her off."

My whole body starts to shake. "But I wanted to protect her."

"The way you protect her is to stay quiet. The way you protect yourself is to win this competition. Trust me, the winner will get the best prize out there."

"What is it?"

"It's something special."

"Freedom?" I ask hopefully.

She casts her eyes down. "You will never have freedom."

My heart sinks and I look down at the floor. But she brings her finger to my chin and pulls it back up. My eyes meet hers.

"The next round is the cocktail party. They will be watching your every move. They will try to surprise you, but you need to surprise them instead. Impress them. Intrigue them."

I nod as if I understand what she means.

"Carry yourself with confidence. Put your shoulders back and hold your head high. You are here and you are in charge. Make yourself believe that and they will believe it, too."

I nod again. As she turns to walk away, I reach out to her.

"What's your name?" I ask.

"Mirabelle."

"Why are you helping me?"

"Because I was once a girl just like you. Alone. Lost. But strong. Willing to do anything to stay alive."

*A*s I enter the hall, I go directly to the bar.

I can't bear to talk to a single person, let alone flirt or smile, if I don't have a drink.

After ordering a glass of wine, I sit down on the stool, keenly aware of the fact that I'm not wearing any panties. No one gave me a replacement pair after what happened on stage.

The rest of the contestants scatter around the room to talk to men in tuxedos, but I need a few moments to myself.

How much do they know about what's really going on here? I have no idea.

Are they all excited to be here like Alessandra is?

Or are some of them like me, someone who has seen glimpses of the truth?

I am not naive enough to think that I have learned the whole truth about this place. I have seen their lavish cell, the dungeon, and one in between, but deep in my heart I know that there is so much that I haven't seen yet.

When my drink is ready, I take a few sips and try to put together a strategy.

Should I make my way around the room and meet some people or should I sit here and wait for someone to come to me?

There are pros and cons to either approach.

If I circulate, then I'm in control. I can come and go as I please.

But if I sit, I can also look around the room and get more of a feel for what everyone else is doing.

I take another sip of my drink and turn slightly on my stool.

That's when I spot him.

A murky figure out in the distance.

I recognize him immediately.

It's almost as if I can smell him.

Can he smell fear in return?

I turn toward the bar and wait.

Then it occurs to me.

I need an element of surprise.

When he touches me, I turn around with a smile.

I flutter my eyelashes.

I flirt.

Scared of Abbott?

Oh, of course not.

I'm happy to see him.

He says something to me. I say something back.

We are bantering. Joking.

Like acquaintances trying to become friends.

I can tell by the expression on his face that he's confused.

But also impressed.

Perhaps, she is happy to see me, he is probably thinking.

Men like him are so arrogant that there's no room in their minds for common sense. Why would I be happy to see him? Why aren't I angry? Is he really this charming? I'm sure that he thinks he is.

But then...something else.

I take a sip of my drink as soon as I see him.

Alcohol isn't the best thing for clearing one's mind, but it's the only way I can take a moment for myself.

What is *he* doing here?

Easton.

I remember him immediately.

He's the guy who tried to warn me.

My fingers start to tremble.

I press them down into the bar to keep them contained.

My jaw clenches.

He's trying to pull Abbott away from me. But why?

If it weren't for my anger, I'd be able to assess the situation better. But when I look at him, all I see is red.

It's him.

That's why I'm here.

He warned me about Jamie, but that was nothing but a trap.

Easton urges me to follow him outside.

He wants to be alone.

A chance to talk.

I don't want to hear it.

I don't want to know him.

I want to get away from him, but something is pulling me toward him.

Perhaps, it's all the hate.

I want to unload on him.

But I can't, can I?

I've pushed the limits of the rules of this place already.

No, I will be poised.

I will stay put together.

Below us, the waves are softly caressing the sand. An idea sparks up in a flash. What if I pushed him over the edge? But am I strong enough?

I take a step forward, but he moves away from the edge.

Just like that, my moment is gone.

He is making amends.

Apologizing.

Trying to convince me that he's not the reason I'm here.

I smile. I nod. I accept his words, but I don't internalize them.

He is a liar.

We both know this all too well.

Suddenly, there's fear in his eyes.

Cameramen are coming.

Soon, our privacy will be gone.

Soon, we won't be able to talk like this.

Wait a second, what does that mean? Is that fear in his eyes? No, it can't be.

Glancing back at the approaching cameras, he tries one last time. I look deeply into his eyes.

They can't hear me yet.

We are alone.

This is my chance to tell him the truth.

I take a deep breath.

"I'm done with this place. With the games you all play," I hiss under my breath.

He says that he doesn't play games, but we both know that's a lie.

"You're playing the hero," I say. "You are pretending to help me so you can rescue me. But not before betraying me at the end."

He looks hurt, but that's just another game.

When the cameras surround us, I take his hand in mine and squeeze it as hard as possible.

Then I look deep into his eyes and thank him for his kindness.

Lying was never anything I could ever do well.

But thanks to my time in York, I'm developing all sorts of new talents.

I'm becoming quite an actress.

If they want to see a show, then a show is what I'll give them.

They haven't seen anything yet.

I pull my hand away from him and spin on my heels.

Holding my head up high, I walk away.

As soon as I take a few steps, I feel sick to my stomach, but I don't dare show a bit of my queasiness.

I lift my chin higher to the ceiling.

This is my runway.

I relax all the muscles in my face and carry myself with grace and composure.

Cameras disperse around me as I walk back, and I realize that Easton isn't the only person I need to worry about.

Everything that's happening here is being recorded.

For someone.

And shown.

To someone.

But who?

EVERLY

WHEN I MEET A GIRL...

$\mathcal{C}$ocktail hour comes to a close as soon as I return. The men quickly disappear and we are told to follow two servants in black gowns to a large lobby area just outside of the cocktail area.

The floors are marble and there's an enormous winding staircase snaking its way to the second floor.

In the middle of the hall, there's a vast round table with a huge bouquet of flowers.

A man in his mid-forties wearing an elegant tuxedo stands near the table. His hair has hints of gray, and it doesn't budge an inch as he moves and talks. He has a soft, effeminate voice with a hint of a Hugh Grant-type of English accent.

"Welcome. Welcome," he says as we crowd around him.

He takes a few steps up the staircase so he can see over all of us.

"Welcome to your home," he says when our voices die down. "My name is J. Like the letter."

The women around me exchange significant glances with each other.

"Just the letter, isn't that mysterious," one of them whispers.

Oh, if you only knew, I want to say.

"You will find your bedrooms upstairs and the kitchen, dining room, and living room downstairs," J continues. "Your suitcases are already in the upstairs rooms, the ones which have been assigned to you. You are very privileged to make it to the Elite and we are happy to have you. I know that the showing and the cocktail party was a little stuffy, so we hope you enjoy tonight's party a little more and let yourselves go."

The Elite?

What's the Elite?

J leaves and I follow the rest of the contestants upstairs. One of the last doors on the left is marked "Number 19." I assume this is meant for me.

Inside, I find a lavish suite.

Large television.

Floor-to-ceiling windows onto a tropical garden.

A large claw-foot bathtub.

A glass shower with four shower heads.

A walk-in closet.

I don't have a suitcase, of course, so instead I find a closet stocked with the same clothes that had once hung in my first room here.

Running my fingers through the dresses, a loud knock startles me.

I place my hand on the knob and I'm pleasantly surprised by the fact that the door actually swings open. A girl about my height with plump cheeks and excited eyes is standing on the other side. She introduces herself as Paige and jumps on my king-size bed.

"Isn't this place just amazing?" Paige announces. Her exuberance reminds me of Alessandra's and I wonder if they both heard about this place from the same person. I mean, what am I missing here?

"Yeah, it's pretty...impressive," I mumble.

"Are you just not dying that you're here?" she squeals, jumping further up my bed and beating her feet against the covers.

"No. I am, I am," I lie.

I really wanted a few minutes alone to gather my

thoughts before the next thing happens, but I guess I know that I won't be able to get her out of my room without a significant effort. She's not one to take a hint.

"What do you think is going to happen next?" Paige asks, wrapping her hands around her knees and looking up at me with large puppy dog eyes.

I shrug. I have no idea. Except that it's probably nothing good.

"So, where are you from?" I ask.

"New Jersey, but I went to school in Ithaca, New York."

"Cornell?"

"Nope, I didn't get in. Ithaca College."

The only thing I know about Ithaca is that it's a particularly cold area of upstate New York.

"My boyfriend went to Cornell, so I thought, hey, Ithaca's a good school. Why not?"

"How did that end up?"

"Well, I'm here, aren't I?" she asks, coyly.

As we continue to chitchat, I quickly realize that Paige isn't as stupid as she pretends to be. She's actually quite observant. I'm not sure what the ditzy act is all about, but I'm eager to find out.

She majored in Anthropology and started a

company that sources crafts made by indigenous women and sells them to fancy boutiques.

"People nowadays really want authentic things, so that's what we are offering them. Plus, a portion of our profits goes to help the women who make the crafts. So far we have craftswomen from India, Haiti, and Guatemala, but we are looking to expand to other countries as well."

"Wow, that's quite impressive," I say.

She barely looks any older than I am, and yet here she is with a company, a business plan, and a mission statement in place.

As much as I want to hear more about her work, there's a question I need answered even more.

"So, I have to ask you," I say after a lull in conversation. "What are you doing here?"

Her eyes open widely, as if in shock.

I lean in and shrug. She shrugs back. Now, I'm confused.

"Um, because this place is awesome," she finally says.

I catch myself shaking my head before I can stop myself.

"Wait, do you not think so?"

I shrug again. I don't really know how to respond

except that I quickly realize that my response is not the right one.

"Everly, it's such a privilege to be here," she says.

Yes, that's what I keep hearing everyone say, but none of you have had the opportunity to experience the underbelly of this place.

"I mean, I know it's a game and all. But it's not every day that you get to be in the running to meet someone so high ranking."

"Like who?"

"Oh, you don't know?" Paige gasps. "Well, from what I've heard, and these are just rumors, of course, but a royal is looking for a wife. He's very charming and ridiculously wealthy. And he brings women to this island for a little competition. Isn't that why you're here?"

"Yes, of course," I say quickly, but not very convincingly. Paige lets it slide.

"I just wasn't sure about the details. I mean, I heard rumors of course," I add.

This seems to put her more at ease.

I don't expect to make a friend in here, let alone meet someone I really like. But Paige grows on me. Quickly.

There's a way that she is.

Open. Sweet. Kind. Unassuming, perhaps?

It's hard to pinpoint exactly, except that she makes me very comfortable. It's almost like everything about her demeanor puts me at ease with who I am.

"So, how did you...find out about this place?" I ask, choosing my words carefully.

"Well, I've heard about it through the grapevine. Sort of."

"Really?"

"You know how it is. I heard it from a friend of a

friend of a friend. I went to a sorority party at Cornell and met a few girls who knew about this contest. They didn't really know anything, but they'd heard about it. They were debutantes back in prep school, real society types, and this place is known among people in those circles."

My heart sinks.

My only hope was that no one knew what was going on here. And now, I learn this.

"Oh, don't look so disappointed," Paige says. "No one really knows what happens here. It was just a bunch of talk. But once I found out that there's this contest, I really wanted to participate."

"Why?"

"My parents are well off, but you know, they don't have real wealth. I want to make my business work, so I need to meet people with real money. Like people who invest in startups. Plus, if in the process, I meet someone nice, hot, and rich, why not, right? I mean, I'm single. I'm down to meet some sexy men."

"But what if you don't like the guy?" I ask.

She shrugs. "No big deal. Relationships are two-way streets. If I'm not into him, then I have no problem leaving."

A familiar feeling of dread fills my body.

She thinks she will just be able to leave.

No problem.

Like it's a choice open to her. I want to tell her the truth, but I have to physically bite down on my tongue to keep myself quiet.

I can't tell her for a variety of reasons.

One, they've already warned me once.

Two, I don't want the same thing to happen to her that happened to Alessandra.

And, three, I need to find out more about how she got here. If they didn't kidnap her like they did me, then how did they bring her here?

I press her a little more about the details while trying to remain as nonchalant as possible. "So, how did they find out that you were interested in attending?" I ask.

"The debutantes didn't really know anything about this except for what they told me."

"How's that?"

"Well, we all know that there are these elaborate masquerade balls that happen in Venice every year during carnival, but no one really knows what happens there, right?"

I shrug.

"Same thing with this place. They didn't know anyone who was invited. Or anyone who has ever been here. It's all very exclusive and hush-hush."

And illegal, I want to add.

"I gave up on it for a while. I mean, no one knew anything about it; no one I knew anyway."

"Or maybe they were just not telling," I suggest.

Her eyebrows go up. "Perhaps."

"And then I met this guy. This really hot guy. We went out a couple of times. I thought he really liked me."

"But he didn't?" I ask.

"No, he did. But he was really old-fashioned. A real gentleman."

"Why do you say that?" I ask, furrowing my brow.

"I'd broken up with my boyfriend a few months before and I hadn't slept with anyone for a while. So, when we went out a few times, I invited him back to my place, but he never stayed over. It's kind of strange to meet a guy who doesn't want to sleep with you on a first date, you know?"

I nod.

"He kept saying that he had to get back to his grandmother."

Grandmother?!

"Wait, what?" I ask.

"Apparently, he was living with her and taking care of her."

My hands start to shake.

I don't want her to see so I press them into the covers of my bed.

My mind starts to race.

No, no, no.

It can't be him.

I've gone over what happened before I got here again and again.

Easton wanted me to think that it was Jamie.

But that was a lie.

It has to be.

No, no, no.

"What's wrong? Are you okay?" Paige puts her hand on my shoulder and nearly jumps off of the bed.

I take a few deep breaths to try to slow down my breathing. Get a hold of yourself, Everly. Don't freak out.

"Yeah, I'm fine," I finally say. "I'm just a little tired from everything today."

"Yeah, I know what you mean."

I get off the bed and open a bottle of water. After gulping it all down, I turn to her.

"So, do you think he was hiding something?" I ask. "Or do you think he really has a grandmother?"

"I don't know." Paige shrugs. "It was a bit strange.

I mean, we had this great chemistry and then he would just leave me hanging after every date. I thought he would at least come over so we could watch some movies and fool around."

"But he didn't?"

She shakes her head. "I kind of started to think that he had a girlfriend. Maybe they lived together. But then he invited me to this fancy party. I wanted to say no, but he kept insisting, so I finally went."

Fancy party? Like at the Oakmont?

"What kind of party?"

"A big charity ball at the Elliott Hotel in New Haven. It's this ridiculously expensive five-star hotel. I've never been there before. It was gorgeous as you would expect."

A charity ball at a five-star hotel. My heart sinks.

"I was really surprised that Jamie knew anyone who would attend a party like that. I mean, you should've seen the silent auction that they had. People were giving away private plane trips and trips to Europe on their own private yachts."

Paige keeps talking, but all I focus on is that name. Jamie.

WHEN THE PIECES START TO COME TOGETHER...

*J*amie.

Jamie.

Jamie.

His name hangs in the air, as if it were a word bubble in a comic strip. It could be a coincidence, but it's not.

"The Bay Foundation was raising money for their clean water initiative. I wished I could have made a bid, but unfortunately I could barely afford to pay my rent that month, especially after I splurged on that dress from Nordstrom for the event."

Jamie.

A silent auction.

The Bay Foundation.

The Clean Water Initiative.

Everything about her story was identical to mine. Except the ending. I got kidnapped. What happened to her? She would tell me the truth, right?

Wrong.

Of course, she wouldn't. I mean, I'm not. I can't.

"So, what happened after?" I ask.

"Oh, at the end, he was a gentleman as always. Gave me a really hot kiss and said he had to go home to his grandmother. And then that night, I got a knock on my door and a courier delivered this gold box."

"Gold box?" I ask. This is...different.

"Yeah, this large box. I swear, it was about this big." She spreads her arms out to her sides. "It had all of these elaborate carvings on it, and they were embossed in gold."

"What was inside?"

"Crystals. Lots of little crystals, which I later found out were actual diamonds. And inside the larger box, there was a smaller box. This one was covered in lace and had a pearl crown brooch wrapped in golden lace on top. The embellishment was exquisite. The invitation had directions to this private airport in Greenwich, Connecticut, and a jet brought me here."

My mouth drops open. So, she got an invitation to this place. With diamonds. Embossed gold.

"Why do you think you got an invitation?" I ask, trying to hide the extent of my surprise.

"Um, I don't know," she says with an air of whimsy. "I was thinking about that for a while, and I sort of get the feeling that it was because it must have gotten back to someone in charge that I had heard about this place and I was looking for an invite."

What about Jamie?

My mind continues to spin.

In all of my time here, I never suspected him.

I mean, I did briefly but then I quickly put those suspicions aside.

No, it couldn't be him.

It had to be Easton.

But now?

Well, it's pretty clear that Jamie had everything to do with this.

There's no way that we would both have the same story to tell. But there's one question that still bothers me.

Why?

Why would Jamie target me?

Unlike Paige, I've never heard of this place before.

I never wanted to come here.

I never wanted to participate in any sort of contest or competition to win the heart of a man I don't know.

I'm not sure I'll ever get an answer to this question.

"So, what about you?" Paige turns to me. "What's your story? You really had to dig deep to get here, too, I'm sure."

I nod.

Of course. What else is there to say?

But Paige doesn't let me get off that easily. "I want to hear all the details," she insists. "C'mon, please. Tell me. I told you!"

That's true. I have no good reason to not tell her.

So, I open my mouth and start to lie.

"I heard about this place in college," I start. "Just like you. Mainly from the rich girls."

"What is it with those girls? They know everything!"

I smile in agreement.

"Well, I was intrigued, but then we graduated and I moved to Philly."

I pause for a moment, trying to decide whether I should tell her what I know about Jamie.

I like her.

I trust her.

But do I trust her that much?

No, I can't.

I want to tell her more than anything, but I need to protect her.

I learned my lesson with Alessandra.

That's not going to happen to Paige.

The story I tell her has some similarities to Paige's, but the details are different.

There's no Jamie.

There's no Bay Foundation.

But there is a charity ball, which I attended with a friend of mine.

I also received a big gold box with a fancy invitation.

Paige listens carefully and then gives me a warm hug.

"What was that for?" I ask.

"I'm so glad that I've met you," she whispers in my ear.

EVERLY

WHEN WE HAVE A PARTY...

Somewhere outside my door, we hear a squeal of excited voices. Music starts to blast and people break out in dance.

These are clear signs of a party in its beginning stages. Paige takes my hand and pushes me out of the room.

"I hear guys' voices. Let's go see what kind of eye candy we have downstairs."

I want to stay in my room and go to sleep early, but I know that I have to participate. I've learned so much just from one conversation with her.

Who knows what kind of clues some drunk guys can give me about this place? Besides, my stomach is growling and I need to have something to eat.

All the other girls are already wearing their pjs

and sweats and Paige and I are the only ones still in our gowns. I turn around to go change, but Paige pushes me toward the kitchen.

"If we don't eat something now, who knows if it will still be there in a few hours. I mean, look at these girls."

The girls, rather, the women, are going nuts. I haven't seen such letting loose since college. The drinks only started pouring a few minutes ago, but most already seem quite lit.

One is doing a handstand over a keg in the dining room and another is flashing her breasts to a bronzed chiseled man-god with long flowing hair.

In the kitchen, I start to make myself a sandwich, when Paige takes out two red cups and pours some vodka into them with a splash of Sprite.

She hands me one.

I take it out of courtesy, but I have no intention of drinking.

Besides the fact that I'm not in the mood for vodka, I also know that I need to keep my wits about me.

Paige clinks my cup and downs the whole thing.

I bring my cup to my lips and pretend to take a drink.

Everywhere I look, women are laughing and

having a good time. A tall tan man with broad shoulders and the body of an Olympic swimmer wraps his arms around Paige and gives her a kiss on her neck. She is caught a bit off guard by his forwardness, but then she quickly reciprocates.

Isn't he gorgeous? She mouths to me while his back is toward me.

I nod and give her a thumbs-up.

"There's a hot tub outside," he says, pulling her by the hand. "Come with me."

"Everly?" She invites me, but I shake my head no.

"Oh, c'mon, please," she begs, pouring herself another drink.

"No, I'm fine," I say, but I make a promise to myself to go and check on her in a little bit. She is on her second drink already and the night is young.

As Paige and her hot guy disappear behind the double doors outside, I toss my drink into the sink and fill it up with water.

Dehydrated and tired, I drink the whole cup and fill it up again. Then holding it in my hand, I make my way around the room.

There are more men here than women and they are all walking models from the recent Abercrombie and Fitch catalog. As I watch them flirt and kiss and party with the contestants, I can't help but wonder what's really going on here.

Where did they come from?

And what are they doing here?

Is this really part of the competition?

Maybe these women shouldn't be flirting or kissing these men. I mean, they are here to compete for the heart of a royal, right? The judges must know about this. And if they don't, then they will soon.

I glance down at my cup.

It's not unlikely that they've seen me replace the alcohol with water. If that makes me a bad sport, then I don't care.

I leave the sandwich and make my way to the entryway, the staircase leading up to my room whispers my name.

I don't want to be here.

I don't want to be at this party.

I don't want to flirt with some guys who, though they are quite attractive, are probably part of some elaborate mind game.

No, all I want to do is climb into that comfortable bed and get some sleep.

"Well, hello there, darling." A familiar voice sends shivers down my spine.

I stop in my tracks and try to wish him away.

Unfortunately, without much success.

Slowly, I turn on my heels.

He is standing a few inches away from me. I can smell a strong scent of liquor on his breath.

It makes me want to vomit.

I take a big step away from him.

"Where are you going, honey?" Abbott asks.

His words come out a little slurred.

He goes to grab my hand and misses on the first try.

He is much more inebriated than I had thought.

I glance around the room.

There are two women and a man on the couch in the corner of the room. They are all making out together and it's about to go further. One of the women is undoing his pants and the other one is laying him down on his back.

I want to yell out to them to help me, but I doubt they will do a thing. And showing him my fear will only make things worse.

Abbott comes closer to me and runs his fingers up my arm and over to my neck.

My pulse starts to race.

My heart feels like it's about to jump out of my chest.

Abbott takes notice. He places his hand over my breast.

"It's okay, Everly. Calm down. Calm down."

I push him away. "Don't touch me," I say sternly.

"Wait a second! What happened to that flirt who I met at cocktail hour? Am I suddenly too much for you to handle now?"

He's mocking me.

Toying with me.

And there's nothing I can do.

"I'm still her," I say.

I need to buy some time to try to figure something out.

But there's really only one decision to make.

Do I give into him? Or do I fight?

I've fought him before and that didn't end well.

But this is different.

Perhaps, in this competition I'm supposed to resist.

I mean, it's not him that I'm competing for, right?

Before I get a chance to make up my mind, Abbott grabs me by the throat.

His sudden attack throws my body into a state of shock.

As I gasp for breath, he tightens his grip and less and less air gets in.

I try to hit him with my hands, but with him at my throat I feel completely incapacitated.

"If you think I got my revenge on you for what you did to me, you're wrong. I'm going to make you pay, you little cunt. You haven't seen anything yet."

Holding me by my throat, he pulls me to the dining room table and flips me over onto my stomach.

Then he pulls up my dress and spreads my legs open with his.

Hot tears start to run down my cheeks as I realize what is about to happen.

When I try to reach back behind me to grab him, he digs his hand into my hair and slams my head into the dining room table.

WHEN I STOP HIM...

The get-together at the house for the contestants is something new.

It's never happened any of the previous years, but my father isn't one to keep things the same. Change is the way of the world, he likes to say.

The house is stocked with plenty of alcohol and even some drugs and male models are brought in to entice the contestants. "To throw them into heat," as my father calls it.

Contestants don't have to be asked twice. The men come with their six packs, biceps, their charm, and with a little bit of alcohol, the get-together quickly becomes a party.

Abbott and I are expected to participate as well. Of course, Abbott has no issues with this. He's not a person you have to ask twice to attend a lavish event with hot girls who are into skinny dipping.

But me? Well, I dread it.

Even out there in the real world, I avoid gatherings of more than three or four people.

The thundering music.

The loud voices.

The boring stories.

I'd rather spend a few hours talking to someone about something, rather than a bunch of people about nothing.

The only person I'm interested in seeing at all is the one who hates me.

Everly March.

She thinks I'm responsible for her kidnapping and for everything else that happened to her in that dungeon.

The thought of this makes my heart ache.

All I ever did was try to protect her. To give her a way out.

I pour myself a drink. One especially drunken contestant grabs my arm and tries to pull me outside.

"C'mon, let's go into the hot tub. I have to see you glisten." Her eyes light up at the end of the sentence.

"I'll meet you there," I mumble and push her out of the door.

With no intention of following her, I escape to another part of the house in search of some solitude.

I have to be here, but that doesn't mean I have to participate.

Or even enjoy myself.

Cradling my drink and trying to drown my sorrows in it, however, unsuccessfully, I walk through the living room, the dining room, the den, and into another dining room set up in the foyer.

Then I see *him*.

I can't see his face, but I've been his brother my whole life. I can sense it's Abbott.

It takes me a moment to process what's really going on.

He's holding someone down.

Pushing her legs open with his knees.

Her dress is over her hips.

Her arm is pinned behind her back.

She's trying to fight back.

He grabs her head and slams it into the glass table.

The sound of the impact echoes around the room.

"What are you doing?" I grab him by the shoulders and pull him off her.

When he reaches for her again, I punch him in the face. Then, I punch him in the stomach and again in the face.

Stunned, he falls to the floor.

"What the hell are you doing?" he moans, cradling his bleeding nose.

"What are *you* doing?" I ask.

That's a rhetorical question that doesn't require an answer. I know full well what he was doing - attacking her. He was about to rape her.

"She belongs to me," Abbott hisses. "She owes me."

I have no idea what he's talking about. "You don't have a right to do this," I whisper.

"Yes, I do," he moans, holding his nose.

"Not here," I whisper.

I don't think he has the right to do this at all, but this is York. The laws that govern behavior in America don't always apply here.

Out of the corner of my eye, I see the girl pull down her dress and slowly head toward the staircase.

"Hey, hey!" I run over to her. "I'm really sorry that he did that..."

My voice drops off as I realize who it is.

She glances up at me with fear in her eyes.

Her mascara is smudged.

Her eyes are red.

Her lipstick is smeared.

"Everly," I whisper her name before I get the chance to stop myself.

"Thank you," she says.

Her voice is barely louder than a whisper. She walks around me and steps onto the staircase.

I reach out for her.

When I touch her, her whole body recoils away from me.

"I'm sorry," she apologizes.

"No, I'm sorry," I say. "I'm sorry that he did that to you."

"And I'll do a lot worse, you cunt!" Abbott yells. "Next time, my brother won't be there to save you!"

Everly starts to shiver. She wraps her hands around her arms.

"Everly, wait." I reach out to her and grab her hand. She looks at me, waiting for me to say something.

But I don't.

I want to take back everything that just happened. But I can't.

"Please, can I go?" she asks.

I nod and let go of her hand.

She gives me a brief nod and disappears upstairs.

Sitting outside of Father's office, I feel like I'm in fifth grade again waiting in the principal's office. Abbott was called in first. I have no idea what he's saying to him, but I'm pretty certain it's an elaborate story of how none of this was his fault.

After he has been in there for close to twenty minutes, Mirabelle comes out and calls me in. I take a deep breath and follow her inside.

Abbott is standing with his arms by his sides and his head hanging low.

From personal experience, I know that this is the best way to take a lecture from our father. Never make eye contact and look as humble as possible.

"Abbott told me what happened tonight," my father says.

He is sitting behind his desk. A large book is open before him and steam from his tea is rising. His pajamas are covered with a silk dress robe.

"And I'm sure it was all true," I say with a tinge of sarcasm.

"What was that?"

I did the right thing. I have to make him see that.

"He attacked a girl," I say. "He was going to rape her in front of everyone. He slammed her head against a table, sir."

"And you came in, pulled him off her, and punched him three times. Is that correct?"

I nod. He waits.

"Yes, sir."

Sir. That's how I've referred to my father ever since I could talk. He has never been anything but a sir to me.

My father thinks that the word represents respect. But respect is the last thing I feel for him.

A long time ago, I made a promise to myself that if I were to ever have a child of my own, he or she would never call me by that despicable word.

"You shouldn't have done that," he says after a moment.

I shrug.

"Do you not agree?"

"No, sir."

EASTON

WHEN HE'S PUNISHED...

*S*tanding before my father, there are many things that I want to say to him about what just happened.

No, I don't think a woman should be raped in the middle of the dining room.

No, I don't think a woman should be raped at all.

But, of course, I can't.

"You may be right." My father waves his hand. "But you had no right to attack your older brother like that."

"He wouldn't remove himself when I asked him to, sir."

"It wasn't just some girl, Father," Abbott interrupts. "It was Everly March. The same bitch who attacked me before. The one who was sent to the dungeon."

"So you were doing what exactly? Trying to exact revenge?"

"I don't know." Abbott shrugs. "Maybe. Mainly trying to fuck with her."

"Well, Easton is right about one thing," Father says with a sigh. "You cannot do that kind of thing in front of everyone. We don't want them getting spooked and ruining our fun."

What an asshole, I say to myself. What a sociopath!

"I wasn't planning on that, but she just wouldn't cooperate," Abbott says.

"Be that as it may, you will be punished for this."

"What?!" Abbott gasps. Even I take a step back.

"You have been taking a lot of liberties with things lately, Abbott. Do not think that anything you do around here goes over my head. There are eyes and ears everywhere."

"But, Father—" Abbott starts to say, but our father raises his index finger and he immediately shuts up.

"No. I don't want to hear it. You will go to Hamilton and spend a week there, learning your lesson."

Hamilton?

Over this?

I guess he really must've pissed him off.

Hamilton is the island closest to York. It's a secret prison which houses people who have wronged my father and people who work for him. I've never been there before and neither has Abbott.

Abbott's face twists in despair. "I'm sorry, I really didn't mean anything—" he starts to say.

"Okay, let's make that eight days then instead of seven," Father says. "Do you care to make it nine?"

Abbott is about to protest again, but he closes his mouth and hangs his head.

"Good," Father says, marking something in his daily journal. "Now, as for you, Easton."

I take a deep breath.

"You seem to have a particular interest in this girl, number nineteen," he says, reading from his journal. "Can you tell me why?"

I don't know the extent of what he knows. He may or may not know what I did at the Oakmont. The key is to not lie.

Even though he is someone who wears so many faces to the world, there's nothing he can't stand more than a liar.

"I had no idea that it was Abbott or who the

woman was. All I saw was a person in trouble and I wanted to help her."

"Why?"

"Because I don't think it's right, sir."

"What's not right?"

"To force women, or men, to do anything that they don't want to do. Sex should be something people do consensually, sir."

"Yes, I would agree with that," my father says, swirling in his chair. "But consent isn't cut and dry like that."

I shake my head slightly, unsure of what he is referring to.

"As you grow up, you will learn that most people out there will do anything and everything for you if you think you can do something for them in return and will do nothing for you if they think you are worthless to them."

I look down at the floor.

"You do not agree, Easton?" he asks.

"I don't want to be disrespectful, sir."

"You are entitled to your opinion, son. And I welcome opposing viewpoints."

Well, that's a lie, but okay, I think to myself.

"The thing is that it was pretty clear back there

that she did not want Abbott touching her and he was forcing himself on her anyway."

"Yes, of course," my father says, waving his hand. "Abbott has terrible manners and a bad temper. But we were talking about consent, were we not?"

"I'm not sure what you want me to say," I say after a moment.

"Do you not agree with me about the fact that a person, not just a woman, would consent to just about anything for the right price?"

If he wants to hear my opinion, I will give it to him.

"I wouldn't call that consent, sir," I say after a beat.

"You would not?"

I shake my head. "If there's a price involved, if he, or she, is afraid, then it's not really a consensual act."

"There are things I do not think you quite understand about relationships, son," my father says.

I hate the way he says the word son. He holds it in his mouth for a few moments, mulls it over, enjoys it before spitting it out.

"And I'm not just speaking about romantic relationships. It's all relationships. There is always a trade. There's always a power struggle. There's always something that someone wants that you either concede or exchange for something else."

I nod, as if I agree.

"You do not look like you agree." He pushes me.

I take a deep breath.

I should not let him goad me.

I should just let this go.

"No, I don't agree with you, sir. Exchanges, money, and power plays are not what relationships are about. Not good ones anyway. Good relationships are based on honesty and respect. Trust."

"You really don't know anything about life, do you?" my father asks after a moment.

"No, he doesn't," Abbott pipes in. "I told you he was an idiot."

I feel anger starting to rise up from the pit of my stomach, but I take a deep breath and keep it at bay.

Why did I expose myself?

Why did I tell him the truth?

Why didn't I just go along with what he said and take his imparted kernel of wisdom and shove it up my ass where it belongs?

WHEN I'M PUNISHED...

"You have an interesting way of thinking about things, Easton," Father says, writing something in his journal. "Unfortunately, I think that you still have a lot to learn."

"I thought that I was entitled to my own opinion, sir?" The words escape my lips before I can stop them.

Shut up, Easton. Shut the fuck up.

"Well, you are. And I've listened. But your opinion indicates to me that you are not fully understanding the world in which we live. And, as your father, I must remedy that immediately."

You mean the fucked up world in which *you* live.

Life isn't really like it is here.

This isn't reality.

This is hell.

"Easton, your punishment is to have sex with number nineteen."

"What?!" Abbott ignites with anger. "I'm sent to Hamilton and he gets to have a romp with that cunt?"

"Yes, Abbott. And, please, do not speak to me in a raised voice. I will not ask you again."

"But why, Father? Why?" Abbott pleads. "It's not fair."

"It is fair. You have a bad temper and you tried to rape a girl in front of all of our guests. We do not do that here, Abbott. You know that. And your brother here, well, he seems to have this confusing idea about what sex really is. Sex is an exchange of power, son. And the sooner you learn that, the sooner you will be released."

His words don't really sink in.

I've heard them, but I don't understand them.

The thing about my father is that he has all of these lessons he tries to teach everyone. And if you have your own idea of how to do things, your own opinion about what is right and wrong, he doesn't care.

If you don't agree with him, then you haven't learned your lesson.

There's no use in fighting him on this. It will only make things worse.

He has said his piece and called Mirabelle. She is waiting in the doorway.

The conversation is over.

"What the hell is he thinking?!" Abbott roars at me as soon as we are outside. I shrug.

"You're such an asshole. I can't believe you get to do the one thing I want to do, and I have to do time at Hamilton. If you don't think you're the favorite after this, then you're seriously delusional."

I shrug again and speed up my pace. I want to get away from him to try to figure this out, but he catches up to me.

"What do you want with her? Do you have a crush on her or something?!" he roars into my ear.

"No, I just don't want you to hurt her," I say, pushing him away from me.

"Well, I will. I promise you that. That cunt has it coming and I'm going to make her pay. Hard."

I clench my jaw.

I've never seen such rage in his eyes before.

Something about Everly is really riling him up. It's like she has this power over him.

I wonder if it's the same thing that's making me risk everything to help her.

We resist the temptation to fight because we know that will only make things worse for us. Instead, we square off and glare at each other, waiting for the other to back down even an inch.

"Hey! Don't forget your orders!" Mirabelle raises her hand, waving the paperwork.

Signed and sealed by the King.

Now, it's official.

We listen to the clicking of Mirabelle's heels on the parquet floors, getting louder and louder with each step. Neither of us moves a muscle until she is standing right next to us.

"C'mon, snap out of this," she says, shaking us by the arms. "You don't want to make this worse."

She hands us each a typed up envelope with the House of York seal in the middle. We take the envelopes and take off in different directions.

WHEN I GET to my chambers, I open the letter. It's printed on lavish scented paper with a House of York seal at the top and Father's signature and stamp at the bottom. This is a lot more official than I had expected him to go.

EASTON YORK HAS three days (72 hours) to have sexual intercourse with contestant number 19 for at least twenty minutes. Both parties are required to reach a climax. Additional parties are welcome to participate in the act, but their presence is not required.

Number 19 is to not know about this order.

If the parties do not consummate the act within seventy-two hours, then Easton will receive two weeks of hard labor at Hamilton and number 19 will be eliminated from the competition.

WHEN I FINISH READING, I want to spit on his signature, but I don't. Everything is recorded.

My own father is forcing me to have sex against my will. Even if I can seduce her, it's not really consensual because I don't want to. I have not been with anyone since...no, I still can't talk about it.

But what choice do we have?

It's not the two weeks at Hamilton that worries me, though they will not be any walk in the park.

It's the fact that if I don't do this, she will be eliminated from the competition. An elimination means there will be an auction and she will be put up for sale. And then who knows what will become of her?

EVERLY

WHEN I WAIT...

*T*he fear of what Abbott just did is still coursing through my veins. I run my fingers over my neck and feel his grasp closing in on me.

Every time I blink, I feel his body on top of mine, pushing my legs open with his knees.

And that scent.

That God-awful scent, which came out of every pore in his body. It was some kind of combination of hard liquor mixed with stale cigarettes.

I have to get it off me.

As soon as I get to my room, I take off my clothes and run into the shower. I scrub my body from head to toe to get every last bit of his stench off. The warm water running down my body puts me at ease.

My thoughts turn to Easton.

My savior.

He came out of nowhere. Just as I thought that Abbott would have me for good, he stopped him.

But why? Isn't he the one who is responsible for me being here?

No, of course not. He was telling the truth back there.

I know that now.

I was wrong about Jamie.

He was the one who lured me here. He was the one who lured Paige here, too. He's the evil one.

Easton is...I have no idea what Easton is.

He's an enigma.

For all I know, this could all just be a game to him.

What if he was just pretending to save me?

What if he's playing the role of a good guy while Abbott is the villain? That's possible, but from the shock on his face, I sort of doubt it.

He would have to be the best actor ever.

No, that feeling in the pit of my stomach, you know the one that warns you of danger, tells me that he's on my side.

He's helping me. Or trying to.

After stepping out of the shower and toweling

off, I climb into my big bed and under the covers, I pull the sheet over my head.

The bedding is so soft and luxurious that it feels like I'm lying on a cloud. I turn off the lights and close my eyes.

The events of the night keep flashing through my mind, but I physically force them out.

I'm not here. I'm somewhere far away.

I'm lying in a meadow, on a bed of daises. The horse that I rode here is grazing next to me. There's a blue sky high above my head and the sun is so bright that it's making me squint.

A loud knock on my door startles me out of my deep sleep. I glance at the nightstand and see that it has been more than two hours.

"Come in!" I yell. The door swings open and Mirabelle invites me downstairs.

"Right now?"

"They are doing the first elimination ceremony."

My heart skips a beat.

Elimination ceremony?

"Now? In the middle of the night?"

"Yes," she says, looking at her clipboard.

"I need some time to get ready," I mumble.

"No, you don't," she says, flipping on the light switch. I cover my eyes and sit up. Running my fingers through my hair, I know that it's a complete mess. It has dried while I was sleeping and now has strange untamable crinkles around the crown.

"Nineteen, I'm waiting," Mirabelle says.

I get out of bed and wrap the sheet around myself. I start to head to the closet, but she stops me.

"What did I say?"

"I can't even get clothes or wash my face?" I ask. Or while we're at it, put on some eyeliner and mascara so that I don't look like I do right now.

"No," she says, walking into the room and pulling me out by my arm.

"I don't understand. What's the big hurry? I'm only wearing a sheet for God's sake."

I don't mean to raise my voice at her, but I also don't want to look like crap.

I've seen those elimination ceremonies on reality shows.

The women are always dressed up and they look fucking airbrushed.

"Isn't everyone going to be really dressed up there?" I ask.

"No. Everyone will be exactly as they are. That's the whole point."

That's when it hits me. I don't know the first thing about this place. And I need to stop trying to make what is happening here make any sense with what I've experienced back in my old life.

I follow Mirabelle downstairs with a familiar feeling of dread.

This is the one constant in my life now. Something new is about to happen to me and it's probably not good. The only thing I can do is take in deep breaths and try to relax. Extra tension in my body and soul is only going to make whatever is about to happen that much harder to endure.

A number of contestants are already there, standing in a line.

Just as they are.

Surprisingly, I don't even look the worst. I look like I've just woken up, but most of them look like they haven't gone to bed yet.

The girl to my right is standing in a soaking wet t-shirt and no underwear. The one next to her is wearing ripped yoga pants and a bra.

Most are too drunk to stand up straight and keep wavering from one side to another on their feet.

The ones at the end aren't wearing any clothes at all.

All have smeared makeup and crumpled hair.

Thankful for my bedsheet, I wrap it tighter around my body.

Across the room from us, I see four people behind a large table, which wasn't there before. Without looking at us once, they are shuffling papers among themselves. The two men and two women are all dressed in black business suits and have severe looks on their faces.

Are these the judges? I wonder. They definitely look like it.

J, the host, comes out and clears his throat to get everyone's attention. The judges look up and the contestants try to stand up straight, the ones that can anyway.

"Are we ready?" J asks the judges. They nod.

Then it hits me.

Wait!

No, she's not here yet.

I double check by looking down one direction and down the other at the contestants next to me.

No, she's not here.

No, no, no.

Paige!

Where are you?

I need to buy more time. I need to find her.

Where is she?

No, they can't start without her.

I can't let them.

She's going to be eliminated for sure if she doesn't show up. Right?

But what can I do?

A thousand different thoughts run through my mind all at once.

I have to do something, but I have no idea where to start.

"Wait," I finally yell out before I have even an inkling of a plan. "Excuse me, but not everyone is here."

I glance back at the line of contestants and realize that it's actually not just Paige who is missing. There were more than twenty originally, but now it looks like there are only ten or so here.

"Yes, we know that," one of the male judges says. "That's too bad for them."

"Wait, what do you mean by that?"

"Well, if we cannot find them then they will not be participating in the elimination," the female judge explains.

"Number nineteen, please get back in line. This is highly irregular," the host says.

I step back, but I can't keep my mouth shut.

"I'm sorry, wait, I don't understand," I say.

Of course, I do.

But I keep my hope alive.

Perhaps, if we talk enough then Paige will show up.

"The contestants that do not show up to the elimination are going to be eliminated," the host says. "Now, if the judges are ready, let's begin."

I glance back at the staircase.

Paige.

C'mon, Paige.

Please come.

Please.

Then somewhere in the distance, from the other side of the house, I hear footsteps.

"Wait, I'm sorry, but someone is coming!" I yell out again. "Maybe it's...one of the contestants."

I don't want to announce that there's one that I am particularly interested in.

Everyone turns their heads and waits.

The footsteps get closer, more sloppy, and uneven.

Then Paige appears.

Barely standing on her feet.

I run over to her and help her walk the rest of the way.

She leans on me for support.

"What's going on?" she mumbles, slurring her speech.

"This is the first elimination, honey," I whisper.

"Are we ready now?" J asks impatiently.

"Yes, yes, we are," I confirm.

"I wasn't asking you," he says with a laugh.

He turns to the judges and they give him a nod.

Suddenly, Paige leans away from me and vomits. The others scatter to get away from the splatter.

"Are you okay?" I lean over Paige.

She throws up again.

I pull her away from the puddle.

"I'm going to take her to bed," I say decisively. "She needs to rest."

"She needs to participate in the elimination," J says.

"Is there anything she needs to do? Or are all of your decisions made?" I ask.

"We've made our decisions," one of the female judges says.

"Okay, well, then is it okay if I take her to her room? She really needs to rest."

"This is highly unusual," J starts to say, but the judge interrupts him and tells me to take her away.

I put Paige's arm around my shoulder and help her up the stairs. Everyone's eyes are on us.

Am I making the biggest mistake of my life? Perhaps.

My original plan was to stay low, not draw attention to myself. Until this point, I've succeeded.

But Paige needs my help. What else can I do?

After putting her to bed, I pour her a glass of water and put it on the nightstand. Then I bring over the trash can from the bathroom, just in case she needs it and place it right near her head.

"Thank you," she mumbles, turning away from me.

"Everything's going to be okay," I promise, even though I have no idea if it is.

I walk out of her room and back downstairs, surprised that they have all waited for my return.

"Okay, let's start," J says as I assume my place in line.

He picks up a set of cards from the judges' table and walks over to the podium.

"When I call your number, come up here and take a box."

"Number seventeen," he says.

The girl with red hair and dressed in a bra and panties walks up to him. J hands her a narrow velvet box.

"Please do not open it until I say so," he says, just as she is about to look inside.

He tells her to return to her place and calls the next number.

Eleven.

Contestants all around me get called up and are given a box. Finally, it's my turn.

"Number nineteen," J says with a big sigh.

I walk up to him.

He hands me a velvet box and whispers, "I'm watching you," under his breath.

Shivers run down my spine. But I give him a smile, take my box, and return to my place in line.

"Okay, open your boxes," he says.

My heart sinks and tears start to gather at the edges of my eyes.

He didn't call Paige's number.

"Excuse me," one of the female judges says, calling him over to them.

I watch as J tries to argue with her, but she remains steadfast.

"Okay, then," J says, clearly disappointed. "It appears as though we are not done yet."

With that, he calls Paige's number, number eight.

A sigh of relief spreads through me.

She made it.

We both did.

"You may now open your gifts," he instructs.

Inside my velvet box, I find a delicate sterling-silver bracelet. It's chain linked all around and a delicate flat portion in the front with the words *House of York* are engraved on it. "Welcome to the House of York," the host says.

We all hug each other from excitement. The elimination ceremony is over and we all made it. J tells us that the following few days are rest days for us to relax and enjoy the property.

I let out a big sigh of relief.

That's exactly what I need.

I imagine myself falling into my comfortable bed and sleeping the hours away. It takes all of my energy to not let myself run up the stairs and fall into my bed before anyone else.

I'll be there soon enough, I say to myself.

"Um, excuse me! Excuse me!" J yells when I reach the top of the stairs.

What now?

"Number nineteen, please come see me."

No, no, no.

I shake my head.

No, this isn't happening.

"Number nineteen," he calls me again. "Come here. I know that you can hear me."

The girls disperse around me.

What could this be about?

Is it because I helped Paige to her room?

Is that why?

But they let her stay.

So, why not me?

Why can't they just leave me alone?

"Your presence is being requested in room 212," he says. "Mirabelle will show you there."

WHEN WE GET TO ROOM 212...

*M*y blood runs cold and my fingertips turn to ice. My heart starts to beat so fast, it's about to jump out of my chest.

Who is waiting for me in room 212?

I search Mirabelle's face for an inkling of what's to come. But she remains stoic and expressionless.

"Follow me, please."

I follow her out of the main doors and into the large garden outside.

The air is wet with humidity. For a moment, I lose myself in the buzzing of the insects and the singing of the frogs. As I follow her down a pathway that weaves in between the tall trees and bushes, the leaves of a tall palm tree brush along my arm.

I haven't touched a plant or another living organism, besides the people in this place, since I've been here.

The touch infuses my body with newfound energy.

I pause for a moment to enjoy its rough texture in between my fingers.

In the dark, Mirabelle doesn't know that I have fallen behind. I press the palm leaf in between my hands and inhale its aroma. Droplets from a recent rain roll off onto my fingers.

I glance up at the moody sky and savor the moment.

Somewhere in the distance, a bird chirps and I yearn for her freedom.

If only I were a bird.

Then I could flap my wings and get far away from here.

"C'mon, I don't have all day," Mirabelle says.

"Where are we going?" I ask, fearing the answer.

"You'll see."

I doubt that's a good kind of 'you'll see.'

Few things in this place have been that.

I don't know how long I've been in this place, but it has been long enough for me to forget what real freedom means - to wake up every day and live life on your terms.

Somewhere in the recesses of my mind, I remember what life used to be like and how much I used to dread going to my job everyday.

I thought that I didn't have a choice then.

I thought that I had to go into work.

But did I really? I mean, really?

It was all an illusion.

I thought I was trapped when really I wasn't.

Yes, I needed the job to pay my bills, but I didn't have to have *that* job.

If I hated it so much, I could've quit and found another.

No one forced me to work there.

Not like here.

Oh, what a stupid little girl I was then.

I made up walls for myself, walls that didn't exist.

In reality, the world was mine to take.

My life was mine to live.

If I didn't want to work at Dr. Morris' office, I could've quit.

If I didn't want to live in Philly, I could've bought the first ticket out of there.

I had a bit of savings and I could've taken a bus

anywhere I wanted - Florida, California, Alaska, wherever.

I could've just walked into the first restaurant, coffee shop, or bookstore that came my way and applied for a job there.

Why did I think that I had no options?

Why did I put myself in a corner like that?

Why did I feel like I had to work there just because it's something that I thought I wanted to do?

Yes, it's something I wanted to do. But then it wasn't.

Why was it so hard to say no? To just veer off course.

To trust myself to take a chance?

If I ever get out of here, I'm going to live my life. Really live it.

I'm going to go where the wind blows and do exactly as I please.

Now, I know what real imprisonment is.

This time, it's not just in my head.

"C'mon, hurry up." Mirabelle leads me out of the garden where I want to stay forever.

Just let me be.

Just let me stay here.

I can't go on.

I can't take anymore of what this place has to dish out.

I follow Mirabelle down a winding pathway outside of the garden. A little bit in front us, I see a large manor house built atop a high, broad, grass knoll surrounded by tall palm trees and tropical pine trees.

Its grandeur complements the estate I just left, but on a smaller scale. As Mirabelle leads me toward the double doors, I take a moment to breathe in the air saturated with salt. The ocean must not be far away.

I stick out my tongue to get a taste of it.

I have not stepped a foot outside in a long time, and I don't know when I will be able to be outside again.

A radical thought runs through my mind.

What if I run?

Just go for it?

Mirabelle looks like she's fit, but I know I can outrun her.

I imagine myself taking off and running toward the sand.

What would it feel like to have sand in between my toes again?

"Are you coming?" Mirabelle asks, holding open the door.

I can't run.

Not yet.

It's a stupid move.

My best chance is to stay in the competition and enjoy the freedoms that I do have.

"Yes," I say with a heavy heart and duck inside.

We walk into a spacious living room with a leather sectional couch facing a large television. A large open-concept kitchen is to my left. To my right is an office.

"What is this place?" I ask. "I thought that I wasn't eliminated. Why can't I go back to my room?"

"You weren't eliminated," Mirabelle confirms. "This has nothing to do with you."

I shake my head. I am getting really tired of these games. They don't just play with my head, but also with my body.

"We're here!" Mirabelle yells out.

I look around.

My heart starts to beat fast enough to jump out of my chest.

Who is she saying this to?

Please, don't be Abbott.

Please, please, I say silently to myself.

"Everly?" A quiet voice breaks my concentration.

I had closed my eyes.

When I open them, I see him.

He's dressed in jeans and a casual gray t-shirt, just tight enough to accentuate his muscular physique.

His hair is slicked back and wet.

A towel is draped over his shoulder.

I take one step back and then another one forward. I let out a big sigh of relief.

"I'm leaving now," Mirabelle announces and leaves before I say another word.

I turn to Easton.

I'm relieved that it's not Abbott for a variety of reasons, but most of all because I kind of like Easton.

He has this quiet, mysterious quality to him.

I've made a lot of assumptions about him and they have all turned out to be false.

He plays his cards close to his chest and that intrigues me.

"What am I doing here?" I ask.

Easton walks away from me. His bare feet leave little impressions on the parquet floors.

"Where are you going?" I follow him, adjusting the sheet around my body.

I should've figured out a way to make this sheet more of a real garment by now, God knows, I've been wearing it long enough.

He disappears into a large room with floor-to-ceiling windows and a view of a pool. It's dark out, but the pool is lit up.

The crystal blue water is calling my name.

"Easton?" I walk into the bedroom.

There's a large California King bed in the center and Easton is nowhere to be found. I'm reluctant to follow him further into his room.

A few moments later, he emerges with a pair of yoga pants and a t-shirt.

"I thought maybe you'd be more comfortable in these," he says. "You can change in there."

I don't have to be asked twice.

I grab the clothes and disappear into the bathroom.

As I put on the clothes, I spin around to get a better look at the place. To say it's luxurious would be an understatement.

I've never seen a bathroom with its own sitting area and a chaise lounge inside of it. There's a large glass bathtub in the middle, right in front of a glass window which spans the whole side of the room.

It offers privacy because it looks out onto a thick tropical forest.

When I come out, I expect Easton to be sitting on the bed waiting for me. But he's not. I walk back into the living room.

Again, I don't see him.

"Easton?"

"Easton?"

The refrigerator door, disguised as just another cabinet, closes and he emerges from behind it.

"Do you want anything to eat?" he asks.

I nod.

"I'm making scrambled eggs."

"I'd love that."

He cooks in silence.

I pour myself a glass of orange juice and wait.

Of all the things that I expected to be waiting for me here, I did not expect this.

When the eggs are ready, Easton carefully gives me a generous portion and we dig in.

"So...what am I doing here?" I ask, devouring my plate.

"Still hungry?"

I nod, feeling slightly embarrassed by this fact. He just shrugs and pulls out a box of bagels.

"Fresh bagels right from my favorite bakery in Brooklyn," he says. "I have them delivered here. Want me to toast them?"

I nod and grab the cream cheese from the fridge.

"You have them delivered here?" I ask as we wait for them to pop out of the toaster.

"My father has money to burn," he says. "I don't take advantage of many amenities here, so I see this as something that he owes me. At least, during my stay."

I spread a generous amount of organic cream cheese on the bagel and take a big bite.

"Wow," I mumble. "This is delicious."

He gives me a nod.

For a few moments, we eat in complete silence. I

realize that it's the first time I've felt completely at ease since I've been here.

I want to ask him a million questions, but I hate to ruin the moment. So, I enjoy it instead.

"Can I make you some tea?" he asks.

I nod.

He puts the electric kettle on.

When the water starts to boil, he flips on the stereo and gets so close to me that I can feel his breath on my lips.

"I'm sorry that you're here," he whispers. "But you have to believe me, I didn't trick you. I tried to protect you."

"I know," I whisper.

I can barely hear myself over the music, and I'm definitely enjoying standing so close to him.

"One of the girls I talked to told me an almost identical story about that guy, Jamie, who took me to the Oakmont," I add.

Easton nods and looks down at the floor. There's a sadness and a vulnerability in him that's irresistible. I dig my fingers into the kitchen island to keep myself from reaching over to him and pressing my lips onto his.

"That's not his real name," he mumbles.

"I know."

He gazes into my eyes. I focus my eyes on his and we get locked in a moment.

He is the first to look away.

"I have to tell you the truth," he finally says, returning his piercing eyes to mine. I wait.

"I thought you still hated me. I'm glad you don't."

"Who said I don't?" I ask with a smile.

He laughs.

I exhale deeply and all of the tension that I've been carrying on my shoulders vanishes. Easton isn't like the rest of them.

There's a humanity in his eyes.

A softness.

He's a stranger here just like I am.

The kettle turns off and Easton lowers the volume of the music. He pours me a cup of tea.

I take a sip and give him a little smile.

Who is he?

Why is he helping me?

"Prince of York, please pick up," a voice says over the intercom.

*P*rince of York? I look at Easton in disbelief.

No, it can't be.

Not him.

He's part of this horrible place?

Perhaps I was wrong about him. I should've gone with my first instinct. I can't trust anyone here.

"Not now, please," Easton says.

"I'll leave your wine right out here, sir," the person on the other end says.

"I should've known it," I say, shaking my head.

"What?"

"That you...you're too good to be true. You are just like the rest of them, aren't you? You were just pretending to be a nice guy. But now you got us wine and you were, what were you going to do exactly? Get me drunk and then do what Abbott tried to do?"

Easton inhales deeply and walks away.

Again, I'm taken aback by his actions.

I expect him to come over to me and try to convince me of something, but he doesn't. I watch as he walks over to the front door and brings in the wine that the waiter left there.

There are two bottles. One red and one white.

I can't see the labels, but I'm sure that they are expensive and extravagant just like everything else is here.

"Are you going to answer me?" I ask.

"You are a little bit confused about your place here," he says after a moment. His tone is severe and unrelenting.

"Yes, my name is Easton. Yes, I am the son of the King of York. What else do you want to know?" he asks, opening the bottle of red.

I stare at him.

"So... was that all an... act? Before?"

"No."

I want more than a one word answer, but I'm not sure if I'm going to get it.

"What am I doing here?"

"I can't tell you."

"What can you tell me?"

"That I'm not going to hurt you."

I nod, but I'm not sure if I believe him.

"Would you like a glass?"

"No," I say too quickly.

"Suit yourself," he says and pours one for himself.

Then he takes it to the living room and sits down on the couch. Unsure as to what to do, I follow him there. I have so many questions and he's the only person who has the answers.

"Is Abbott your... brother?" I ask slowly. I sit on the edge of the chair as far away from him as possible.

"Unfortunately."

"Is he also a Prince?"

"Yes."

"What does this title mean?"

"On this island, it means everything. Out there, in the real world, I don't know. Not that many people know about this place. And the ones who do like to pretend that they don't."

We sit in silence for a few minutes.

He turns his head away from me and looks out the window wistfully.

For a moment, I get the feeling that he's as much of a prisoner here as I am.

Who are you Easton of York?

But then he turns toward me and gives me a stern glance. His dark almond eyes narrow and his jaw clenches. There's anger behind them.

Discontent.

Is it directed at me?

Or is something else bothering him?

I have no idea.

"What is this place, Easton?" I ask in a whisper.

I want to talk to him frankly, but I know that we can't. Someone is listening and I don't know him well enough to understand the subtleties of his metaphors, let alone his silence.

"This is the Kingdom of York," he says after a moment. "There are no rules here. Well, there are lots of rules, but no rules as to what can happen to...you."

That sentence sends shivers through my body.

"But I suspect that you know that already," he adds.

"And what about you?" I ask.

He stares at me with his cold dark eyes.

Is this the man who just saved me?

Is he the one who fought off his brother?

Or did I imagine all that?

These and a million other questions run through my mind, but they all circle around one.

Who are you, Easton?

Who are you really?

"What about me?" he asks.

"Are you too good to be true?" I ask.

I do my best to fill the question with as much emotion as possible. It's more of a pleading than anything else.

"I don't know what you mean," he says, categorically. "But I will tell you one thing. I am not your friend."

I shake my head. For some reason, this hurts me to my very core.

"I didn't expect you to be," I say as nonchalantly as possible. "So, what is this competition about?"

"I'm not at liberty to tell you."

"So, what are you at liberty to tell me?"

"I can tell you things about me, if you want," he volunteers.

I nod.

"I don't live here. I live in New York. I am here only out of...obligation."

"What do you mean?" I ask.

"I'm required to be here. And though I'm not

your friend, I don't want you to think that I'm like...them."

I narrow my eyes.

What is he referring to?

Does he know what's going on here?

Especially in the dungeon? I want to ask, but I can't bring myself to.

Plus, I'm pretty sure that he will lie if I ask him directly about it.

And I don't think I can handle another lie. Not from him. Not now.

So, instead I ask him something that I don't think he will lie about - his life. He tells me about his job as an investment banker at a rival firm to the one that his father runs.

"So, how's New York?" I ask.

"Expensive."

I look around. "Seems like your family has plenty of money."

"I don't take any money from my father," he says sternly.

"Except for bagels," I point out. This breaks the tension on his face and a little smile emerges at the corners of his lips.

"Yes, I guess except for bagels."

"So...tell me something else that's...true," I ask.

He takes a moment to think about it.

"I want to get to know you better."

This makes me sit back in my chair. A little stunned.

"You do?"

"Yes."

"Why?"

"Because I've wanted to get to know you ever since I first saw you," he says.

He's leaning in toward me now.

The restrained expression on his face is all but gone.

It is not lost on me that he doesn't mention the Oakmont. I know now that what happened there was not a sanctioned event.

He went out on a limb to help me, to warn me about Jamie, but it wasn't enough.

Oh, how I wish I had run away from there the second he talked to me.

Maybe then I stood a chance of getting away.

"Is that why you helped me?" I ask.

His jaw tightens.

His irises dilate and he gives me a little shake of the head.

His eyes plead for me to stay quiet.

So, I clarify.

"Is that why you helped me when Abbott attacked me?"

He exhales deeply - a sigh of relief.

"No," he says.

"Really?" I don't believe him.

"I didn't know it was you. But he shouldn't have attacked anyone like that. I would've helped any woman in that situation."

"Well, in any case, thank you for helping me," I say. "Thank you for...everything."

"You're welcome."

The subtext of what's going on in our conversation and in all the pauses of what is left unsaid could fill an ocean.

We don't know each other well, but I can feel it somewhere deep within me that I get him. And he gets me.

We talk long into the night about anything and everything.

We avoid the topic of York because the truth can't really be told and sometimes it's too hard to talk in spaces and ellipses.

He asks me about my life in Philly and I tell him about college and work. More about what I really enjoyed (college) and less about what I didn't (work).

The hours seem to float away as we talk and I try

to remember the last time I talked like this with anyone before.

"You must be exhausted," Easton says after I yawn.

"No, I'm fine," I start to say, but then another yawn comes out of nowhere.

"Why don't we go to sleep?"

Before I get the chance to respond, Easton says he'll take the couch and leads me to his bedroom.

"I can't take your bed," I say. "I can just sleep out there."

"No, you're my guest," he insists. He goes to his closet and retrieves a pillow and a blanket. "I'll be fine. You get some rest."

I'm about to protest, but he insists.

Too tired to argue, I climb into his large bed, which is big enough for both of us.

I know that I should insist on him coming back here, but my eyelids get heavy and suddenly I don't have the energy to lift them.

EVERLY

WHEN I TAKE A DIP...

*T*he following morning, Easton says he will be back in a few hours and leaves me alone. I glance out of the window at the sparkling pool.

It's calling my name.

I don't have a swimsuit, but it doesn't matter. I grab a towel and go outside. I don't remember the last time I have been in a pool.

When I was a kid, we used to go on a weeklong vacation to a two-bedroom rental near Sarasota, Florida. My parents would save up money and I would look forward to that one week all year long.

It was walking distance to the beach, but not too close, so dragging our stuff there every morning was a bit of a chore. Summer is low-season, and it rains a lot. It doesn't fall all day long, but you just never know when you're going to get rained out.

After a morning at the beach, floating around in the bathwater of the Gulf and playing in the sand, we would retire to the condo for the afternoon to have lunch and wait out the rain.

If the rain stopped quickly, I'd beg my parents to go back. But they'd often resist, preferring instead to lay on the couch and watch TV. I couldn't go the beach by myself, so I'd have to satisfy myself with the community pool.

I'd peel on my wet bathing suit, grab my damp towel, and jump into the pool. Hardly anyone was ever there in the afternoons, right after the rain, and I would pretend that it was all mine.

When I grow up, I'm going to get a house with my own private pool and never miss a day of swimming, I remember promising myself.

As I dip my toes in the blue water, all of these memories flood back.

The smell of chlorine.

Eating watermelon with wet hair in front of the television.

The cool of the air conditioning after a hot day outside. It felt so cold against my skin that I'd wrap myself up in an old sweatshirt just to stay warm.

I descend into the water.

My long hair takes on a life of its own as it surrounds me.

I let out the gulp of air, watching the bubbles slowly rise to the surface.

The water is warm and comforting.

When I finally come up to the surface, I realize that I'm crying.

What started out as just a little tension in the back of my throat is full out sobs by the time I come up for air.

I fall back under and open my mouth.

Water rushes in and I push it out with the force of my scream.

I scream at the top of my lungs, but I barely make a sound.

I don't know exactly why I'm crying.

I'm not scared or sad. It's something more than that.

The last time I cried like this, I was in college and it was in the middle of finals week. I'd taken three finals that week and I had two more to go.

It felt like the week would never come to an end. Like I would never have my life back. All of the stress, the angst, and the uncertainty finally came to a climax and pushed me over the edge.

And now?

It's kind of like that.

Being here in Easton's house puts me at ease and gives me space to breathe.

But for how long?

The truth is that I have no idea what's going to happen to me *later*.

All I know is that this feeling of peace can't last.

I push off the wall and launch myself through the pool.

I move my body like a fish and when I reach the other side, I do a flip turn, take a breath at the surface, and head back in.

In middle school and high school, I swam on a swim team and was quite good. Breast stroke was my favorite, but there's nothing like a butterfly kick to really make you feel like a fish moving through the water.

I don't bother with my arms.

I'm not trying to go fast.

I just want to glide and stay below the surface for as long as possible. Maybe I won't have to go back up, ever again.

In the water, I lose track of time. It seems to not so much stand still as move in concentric circles.

It's as if time ceases to be linear.

Direct.

Going from one event to another.

My thoughts hop from one memory to another.

One moment, I am floating on my back at twelve years old.

Then, suddenly, I'm in college sitting alone in the library on Friday night. It was on those Friday nights that I thought I was preparing myself for something.

I put so much pressure on myself.

I was so worried that if I didn't study hard and ace every test, every class, and every semester that my life wouldn't turn out right.

Well, that's the thing about life, isn't it?

You never know where it's going to take you.

All that studying and preparation gave me a life that I had no interest in living.

And then suddenly, in one moment, it was gone.

You would think that this experience in York would make me pine for my old life. But in reality, it made me realize how much of a fool I have been.

Instead of going out there and living - making mistakes and putting myself out there - I spent a lot of time being afraid.

I realized a long time ago that I had no interest in that job. Yet, I continued to settle for it.

I settled for a lot of things, including men.

And now, I'm stuck in a place with few options and few choices.

Except I do still have the ability to feel.

So, what do I feel now?

And do I dare explore that further?

I lift my head out of the water and look around.

Outside dining room set.

Poolside lounge chairs.

Palm trees swaying in the wind.

My thoughts drift back to Easton.

The man I never expected to meet.

The man I should not have feelings for.

I don't know much about him yet, but I find myself drawn to him, and not just to his dark thick hair and emerald eyes.

It also has nothing to do with his strong, chiseled body which glistens in the water. Although those things do not hurt.

But my attraction to him goes beyond that.

He's got this gravitational pull on me and the closer we are to each other, the closer I want to be still.

But these are dangerous thoughts to have.

This is York, after all.

I am in a competition for the heart of a man I am yet to meet.

One thing I do know is that it's not Easton.

Or...wait? What if...it is?

I climb out of the pool and dry myself off.

Is this part of the game?

Is this our opportunity to see if we can make a connection?

I take a deep breath and wrap the towel tightly around my naked body. Then I go inside and put on some dry clothes.

The air conditioning feels cold against my skin, so I slip Easton's sweatshirt over the t-shirt and the pajama pants that I find in his closet.

We haven't even known each other for that long and I'm already parading around in his clothes. This isn't good, I think to myself with a smile.

Being in Easton's home, wearing Easton's clothes, puts me at an ease that I haven't experienced in a long time. Not since I've been here.

Perhaps I should not trust it, because it is wise not to trust anything that happens to you in York.

But I cannot help but relax and unwind.

Even if it is a mistake, at least, I have some peace *right now*.

Lying down on the couch and propping my feet up, I am reminded of the old saying about how there is no other moment, but right now.

The past is gone and the future is not here.

Yesterday has expired and tomorrow has not come yet.

The only time is now.

The only real moment is the one that exists, this one.

My eyes fall to the pad of paper sitting on the end table next to the couch.

It's blank. Eager to be filled up with words.

I grab the pen next to it and start to write.

I haven't written anything in a long time and the words just pour out of me.

They are not really a story.

Not yet.

Just thoughts and emotions and a collection of truths that I've experienced since I've been here.

I do not write about the details of what happened to me.

Just what I've felt.

I do not write for anyone in particular.

I write to record my experience.

Perhaps, that's the reason why anyone writes and why anyone reads. We all want to know other people's truths. We all want to learn about other people's lives. And it is through stories that we get what we are seeking. It is through stories that we become human beings.

The words flow out of me like a raging river.

One page turns into two and then into five.

I write until my hand cramps up.

I write until the words become illegible.

I used to think that I needed someone's approval to tell a story. Not long ago, I remember sharing my desire with Jamie and being overjoyed by his support.

But now, I know that I do not need anyone to tell my truth.

Other people do not matter.

What matters is my ability to tell it.

EASTON

WHEN I GIVE HER SPACE...

I did not leave the house for any other reason than to give her space. She has not had space to herself since she has been here and I know she needs it.

And not just any space. She needs a space where she feels safe.

A place where she knows that nothing bad will ever happen to her.

My home will be that place.

When I come back, I look through the window near the front door and see her sitting on the couch.

Hunched over with her legs in a lotus position, she is frantically jotting down her thoughts. I watch as she finishes one page and then turns to the back.

When she's finished with that one, she turns to

the next. Her hand cramps up and she shakes it out and then continues.

What is she writing? I wonder. And why is she so feverishly trying to get it all out?

I stand on the doorstep and wait. I do not dare to interrupt her.

A long time ago, my mother told me that creativity requires momentum. Once you get started, you just have to keep going until you are done or you run out of it.

If you are interrupted or if you lose your place, it is very difficult to get it back.

My mother is dead now, but she loved to write. She never published anything, but she wrote a lot.

I have notebooks and notebooks of her stories and novels.

I don't know if she had ever tried to get them published, but I know that my father did not approve.

"In all fiction, there's an inkling of truth." He likes to say. "Authors try to hide this by pretending that they are just pretending, but the people around them know that some of it is true. We do not need people coming around and reading things into your novels."

And so her work went unpublished, but not unwritten.

A real writer must always write, she told me. If she were to stop writing, she would stop breathing.

When I was little, I spent a lot of time with my mother and she used to tell me these elaborate stories about ordinary boys who fought off dragons and other villains because it was the right thing to do.

I used to go to bed imagining myself fighting those battles. My mother was always someone who had a strong moral compass and it always pointed north.

I don't know what she was doing with my father. Even when I was young, he generally resembled the villain in the story a lot more than the hero.

My mother died when I was only eight.

Back then, my father worked long hours and my brothers and I saw him only one weekend a month. He traveled a lot for work, growing his empire. But her sudden sickness and death made him get more involved in family life.

Unfortunately, for all of us.

Suddenly, it was he who was imparting wisdom to me at nights. And his stories were very different from hers.

His stories were ones about men who fought against all obstacles to take over the world, just for the sake of it.

His stories were ones about men who sought revenge against those who had wronged them, no matter how insignificant those wrongs were.

That's when I started to fear him.

He was not a man who fought for what's right in the world.

He did not fight to make the world a better place.

He only cared about himself and he would do anything to make himself richer and more powerful.

For many years, I was angry with my mother.

I was angry at her for marrying him.

I was angry at her for making him my father.

But I was most angry with her at leaving me with him.

How could she do that?

Didn't she realize how awful he was?

Why did she stay?

Why didn't she leave him and take me with her?

I spent my life trying to find answers to these questions, but I never got any. I doubt that I ever will.

My only consolation was that maybe my father was not the man he once was.

Perhaps, there was a time when he was kind and compassionate and that's when she fell in love with him.

But I sort of doubt it.

In one of her journals, I read a story about a woman from a poor family who had to marry a wealthy duke whom she hated. She hated him at first, but then she broke through his hard shell and realized that he was actually a kind and wonderful man who she fell in love with.

Right? Wrong.

In my mother's story, the woman hated this duke when she married him.

She hated him when he raped her.

She hated him when she bore his children.

She tried to teach her children how to not be like him, and with the youngest one she succeeded.

He was a kind boy who had the ability to love despite his father or his brothers.

But her other children were like her husband - cruel and unforgiving.

And then one day, she got sick and died of a broken heart, leaving her youngest at the mercy of his family.

I found the journal with this story hidden in the false bottom of her trunk.

It wasn't anywhere near any of her other writing.

Hidden and stowed away, it was never meant to see the light of day.

No one was ever supposed to find it.

It was her secret because it was the truth.

It was the truth about the family she'd created and raised.

It was the truth about York.

I KNOCK LOUDLY on the front door when Everly stops writing and puts the pen down.

I wait until she scrambles to hide her paper and pretend that she was watching TV this whole time.

I know that she's not afraid of me for the same reasons that my mother was afraid of my father, but I hate that she is afraid of me at all.

WHEN I TELL HER A SECRET....

I can smell the chlorine as soon as I get into the house and I ask her how she enjoyed the pool. She seems a little embarrassed by the fact that she went swimming, but she shouldn't be. Not at all.

"Please, do as you like. I hardly use that thing at all."

"What? Really?" Everly looks shocked. "Oh my God, if I lived here, I'd be in there day and night. You'd never be able to get me out."

We talk about the water for a little bit. I like the pool, but I prefer the ocean.

Its endlessness draws me in and makes me feel like everything is going to be okay.

I look at the horizon, far into the distance, where

the water meets the sky, and I imagine myself out there bobbing along on my sailboat.

Sailing away from everything.

"I've never been sailing," she says after a moment. "I think I'd like it."

"There's nothing like it. When the wind is just so calm but strong, you set your course and let the world just push you away from...everything. I mean, from all of your problems."

"Most of my problems are from here," she whispers quietly under her breath.

I'm sorry, I mouth the words while covering my mouth with my hand. She looks away from me with a tear gathering at the bottom of her eye.

I want to reach out to her.

Touch her.

Bring her closer to me.

A strand of her hair breaks free from the rest and falls into her face. Before I can stop myself, I reach out and move it out of the way.

Just one touch sends a current of electricity through my whole body.

I haven't felt this way since...well, let's just say it was a long, long time ago.

"So, do you go sailing often?" she asks.

"No, not really."

"Why not?"

"I haven't been in...a couple of years."

"Oh, because of your job?"

I shake my head. I don't know if I should tell her, but the words come out before I can stop myself.

"The last time I went, someone very close to me...passed away."

The word 'died' is still too painful to think, let alone say out loud.

It has been almost three years, and yet the shock and pain of losing her persists. She was so young and I loved her so much.

"How did she die?" Everly asks, taking my hand in hers.

I stare down at her palm and I can't stop the memories from flooding in.

We are sailing in crystal blue waters around the Bahamas. The sun is high in the sky and the wind is blowing through our hair.

We haven't known each other for that long, but we loved each other deeply and passionately.

That weekend we spent making plans.

I was going to run away from this place.

From my family.

From my life in York.

And I wasn't going to just run away to New York.

I was going to change my name, my whole identity.

"What do you mean, change your identity?" Everly asks.

I don't bother lowering my voice. If anyone is listening, they already know the truth. None of this is secret anymore.

"We had plans," I explain. "I was working on getting a new passport. I had saved some money. In a world where everything is electronic and you can track anyone online, the only people who are invisible are the ones who live off the grid completely."

"Where were you going to go?" Everly asks.

"We were just going to sail away. Into the blue, as she called it." I feel a pinch somewhere in the back of my throat.

I swallow to keep the pain at bay. I have mourned her enough, but it never seems to be enough.

"Alicia was willing to go off the grid with me," I continue, clearing my throat. "She was from a wealthy family. Her father was a friend of my father's; he was a CFO in one of my father's companies. But she was willing to give up her whole life to disappear with me."

"Why did you want to disappear?" Everly asks.

There's no other way to answer but to say what is sanctioned by the monarchy. To say the same words that I had previously said in the official apology to the Kingdom of York.

"I was a stupid kid," I say. The tone of my voice changes as I recite the official statement from memory. "I made a mistake. I thought that I could have a better life somewhere else, but I was wrong. I could say that I didn't know any better, but I know that I was just rebelling. Looking for someone to blame for what happened. I regret my decision to do that to this day."

Everly, sensing the change, looks up at me surprised. She is more perceptive than I had thought.

I want to add that the only thing that's true about what I had just said is the last sentence.

I want to tell her that everything else is a lie, something I was ordered to say. But, of course, I can't. A part of me thinks she already knows.

"So, what happened?" Everly asks.

"We thought that we could just sail off into the sunset. We thought that we could just escape, you know?" I ask.

She nods.

"We should've known better."

She waits for me to continue.

"There was an accident. The morning that we took off. The engine caught fire and she got locked below deck."

"Locked?" Everly looks at me perplexed.

"I don't know." I shake my head. "A fire started and I called her name. I tried to open the door, but it wouldn't budge. The fire got worse and worse and the boat started to sink. I called for help, but they arrived too late."

"Oh my God," she gasps. "I'm so sorry."

"I checked the engine the night before. I checked everything and everything was fine. Not just operational, but in excellent condition. And that door? It never had a lock on it. Yet, when the fire started, she couldn't get it open and I couldn't break it."

What I don't say is that I still wake up in the middle of the night hearing Alicia's screams.

She yelled for me to save her, but I failed.

There was nothing I could do.

The door wouldn't open.

What I also don't tell her is that I didn't leave her even when the smoke got too thick. Even when it engulfed me completely.

The water was filling up the cabin, but I kept diving under and trying to save her.

Finally, the last thing I don't tell her is that York's Coast Guard arrived before I ever called them. It was like they knew what was happening all along.

I have my suspicions, of course, about what really happened.

Perhaps, my father had found out about our plan and had Alicia killed. But he had to make it an accident. She was the daughter of one of his closest friends.

Of course, this is just speculation. What proof do I have?

Everly leans over, wrapping her arms around my shoulders.

"I'm sorry," she whispers in my ear.

When she looks up at me, the flutter of her eyelashes brushes against my cheek, and I press my lips onto hers.

EVERLY

WHEN THE FISSURES START TO DISAPPEAR...

There's something about the way he's looking at me.

All of his defenses are down.

He is showing me parts of him that he has held hidden for a very long time. He's dripping in vulnerability, and it's pushing me closer to him. I need to touch him. I need to tell him that everything is going to be alright.

I hate the pain that I see in his face.

I hate the world in which he lives.

I have been here only a short time, and I am certain that this is one of the worst places in the world.

Everything is gold and gilded, yet the darkness still manages to seep out.

The pain that he feels for this woman he loved is all over his face. It hurts him to even speak about it.

In his pain, I see my reflection.

I haven't lost anyone, but I have lost a big portion of myself here.

In this place.

I never thought that I would ever be able to get that part of me back.

But being here, in this room with Easton, I feel something within me mending.

It's like I'm a statue with a fissure running down my side. One bad move can make the fissure crack and I will never be okay again. But, with the right care and tenderness, the fissure might also be filled up. And perhaps, it can disappear completely.

He presses his lips onto mine and the repairing process begins.

His lips are soft and effervescent. At first, they touch me lightly. But after a few moments, they hunger for more. I kiss him back with the same intensity.

After feeling nothing but hate for so long, it is a shock to feel an inkling of love.

He runs his fingers down my spine. I dig my fingers into his shoulders.

He buries one hand in my hair and tugs on it, pulling my head back. My neck is exposed.

He presses his lips and runs his tongue from my ear down to my collar bone.

I moan with pleasure.

He is careful and delicate, yet firm.

I quiver beneath his touch.

I gasp.

I reach for his shirt and pull it off.

His tan skin glistens in the afternoon light and I run my fingers down every muscle in his lean, taut stomach.

His pecs move with each breath, bumping into my fingertips. I laugh when we collide.

"My turn," he whispers, pulling off my sweatshirt and then the t-shirt underneath. My breasts fall open to him and he puts one in his mouth.

He tongues my nipple, taking it carefully between his teeth. I bend away from him in pleasure.

He takes my breasts in his hands, burying his head in between. I laugh. He squeezes lightly and I bend my back even further back.

With one quick motion, he flips me over.

I don't see it coming, but suddenly I'm across his lap with my butt in the air. He pulls down my pants, exposing my flesh.

"What a nice little butt. I just want to bite into it."

He leans down and gives me a big kiss.

A warm sensation starts to build inside of me.

He takes my butt cheeks and spreads them wide. Then he runs his fingers over my clit and around the inside of me.

It feels so good that I have to get away. But he holds me down.

"Where do you think you're going?"

With another swift motion, he slides his body down and pushes me up. Suddenly, my ass is right at his face.

My legs are spread open and he presses his tongue deep inside of me.

His hands move in little concentric circles around my clit and I start to feel woozy from the pleasure.

With my hand resting on his hard stomach, I undo his pants and pull out his large, glorious cock.

I wrap my hand around it and feel it throbbing. When I sink my mouth around it, he moans in pleasure.

With his fingers deep inside of me, I feel myself getting closer and closer to climax.

My breathing is speeding up.

My body starts to tense.

But before I get there, he flips me around and impales me.

His eager cock is waiting for me, piercing through me.

My body closes in around him, taking him deep inside. His hands hold me in place at the waist and we move as one.

My hips move in sync with his moans.

I grab my breasts and squeeze them. He reaches up and puts one in his mouth.

"Come for me, Everly," he says.

I move faster and faster.

"Come for me, now," he instructs.

The power in his voice sends me over the edge. My whole body tightens around him and then a rush of emotion surges through me as if it were an avalanche.

"Ahhhhh!" I scream out as he gyrates his cock in and out of me and moans along with me.

A moment later, I collapse on top of him.

My body is spent.

I don't have an ounce of energy left.

Easton wraps his arms around me and gives me a soft kiss on my lips.

* * *

IN THE MORNING, I wake up next to him. My body is tangled up in sheets. Our legs are intertwined and I'm not entirely sure where I end and he begins.

It has been a very long time since I've had anyone make me feel this good. I'm not just talking about physical satisfaction.

He's definitely an expert, but it's more than that.

A lot more.

I feel myself becoming whole again.

I was a little broken when I found myself here.

They broke me entirely in the dungeon.

But last night was the beginning of a renovation.

"Last night was..." Easton begins to say, but I put my finger to his lips. It was so much more than what can be summed up in one-word.

"Epic," he says, kissing my fingers.

Epic. Huh? I did not expect that.

"Was it not?"

"No, epic seems...appropriate," I say.

We lie together for a few moments, staring at the ceiling.

Oh, how I wish that I had met him under different circumstances.

In a bar, perhaps? Or on a blind date? Or even on a dating app. Anything but here in York during this.

"Was I allowed to do that?" I ask.

"What do you mean?"

"Well, with the competition and everything? I have no idea. I mean, they didn't give me a set of rules or anything. But now I was thinking that maybe this was...out of line."

"I don't think so," he says with a little smile at the corner of his lips.

I look at him, narrowing my eyes.

Wait a second. What's going on here?

"What?" Easton asks.

I sit up and, out of habit, wrap my sheet around me.

"They haven't told us who this mystery person is that we're supposed to be competing for."

"So?"

"So?" I look deep into his eyes. "Is it you?"

Just then the doorbell rings and Easton goes to answer it.

WHEN THE DOORBELL RINGS…

I run after him and demand that he answer me. As he reaches for the door, I jump in front of it and refuse to let him open it.

"Please!" I plead excitedly. "You have to tell me!"

He tries to push me out of the way, averting his gaze. When our eyes finally meet, I see that his are cold and expressionless. Suddenly, I'm sorry that I had brought any of that up.

"I was just joking."

"You'll find out soon enough," he whispers. "That it's not me."

A cold shudder rushes through my body.

It's the tone of his voice. There's fear in it.

Who is it then? If it's not him, then who?

* * *

THE DOORBELL RINGS AGAIN, snapping me out of my daze.

Mirabelle is here. She is telling me to get dressed. I have to attend some sort of meeting. I'm only half hearing the words that are coming out of her mouth. And I'm understanding even fewer of them.

"Go get ready," she says, shaking me by my shoulders. "You have to wear something professional."

"I don't have anything," I start to say, but she hands me a pencil skirt, a light pink blouse, a pair of heels, and a makeup bag.

I want to talk to Easton again, but he is avoiding me. He knows more about this than he is letting on and suddenly I'm angry at him.

Why won't he tell me?

If he can't tell me outright, why can't he tell me in secret?

He can turn up the music and whisper it in my ear. He could write me a note. Anything, but this.

She takes me to the bathroom and watches me change. She applies my makeup and helps me put on the heels.

I come back to the living room, eager to speak to Easton. But he's not there.

Mirabelle points to the pool. Easton is swimming laps.

"Let's go," she says.

"I have to say goodbye."

"You don't have time," she says and pushes me out of the door.

"What's going on?" I ask her. "Why...where are you taking me?"

"You will see."

As we exit Easton's house, I feel a cloud of darkness descend upon my shoulders. The lightness that I felt only a few hours ago is all but gone.

In reality, I am not a free woman.

I'm a prisoner.

A slave.

I don't have any say in anything that happens to me.

Mirabelle leads me to a large door.

It's elaborately carved with scenes depicting people in everyday life.

Some parts of it are scratched up and weathered.

It stands in stark contrast to the rest of the mansion.

"Isn't it beautiful?" Mirabelle asks. "It's Italian. It used to belong to the Medici family."

If it's so old, then shouldn't it be in a museum, not rotting away in the tropics? I wonder to myself. Mirabelle pushes the doors open and leads me into a long hall.

It's dark and empty except for the tapestries hanging on the walls. Light streams in through the stained glass windows.

Somewhere in the distance, I see a chair.

More like a throne.

On it sits a figure - his face and body engulfed in shadow.

Mirabelle leads me toward him. Our shoes make a loud clicking sound as we walk, which echoes all around the chamber.

The throne is a baroque high-back chair upholstered in beautiful plush silver velvet fabric. It boasts rich rolled arms and wood silver-finished legs. Slender and elegant, it has somewhat of a contemporary business look.

The man sitting on it looks to be in his sixties and in good shape for his age.

Mirabelle touches my arm just before we get too close to him.

"Do you know who I am, Everly?" he asks.

I don't really know, but I have my suspicions.

"Venture a guess?" he asks in his soothing, calm voice.

"King of York?"

"That's a good girl." He nods approvingly.

The King is dressed in a three piece suit with cufflinks. I don't know why I'm surprised by this. This is the modern world after all. I've seen plenty of royals in magazines wearing suits and regular dress clothes. Still, it's a bit off-putting.

The King runs his long fingers over the arms of the throne as he looks me up and down.

"Modern people don't have the proper clothes to sit on thrones, do they?" he asks, as if he is able to read my mind.

Not sure how to respond, I shrug.

"It's not like it was back in the day. I mean, I read about these Kings and Queens and their elaborate garb...because, of course, they didn't wear just clothes, they wore garb."

"Yes...sir," I say.

"You don't have anything else to add to what I just said?" he challenges me.

I take a moment to collect my thoughts.

"Well, I guess it's the nature of the world right

now," I say. "With manners and etiquette falling by the wayside, sir."

I lower my head slightly in a respectful nod. Keeping my head in this position, I put my left foot behind my right and shift most of my weight onto the front. Then I lower down, bending my knees outward.

"An unexpected curtsy! Wow, I'm impressed," the King exclaims, clapping his hands. "Only, you want to extend your right foot behind your left. Otherwise, that was perfect execution."

"Yes, sir," I repeat myself and do as he says. He claps louder.

"Well, well, well, Ms. Everly March. You...are full of surprises, aren't you?"

I'm not sure how to answer, so I just interlace my fingers and stand broad-shouldered before him.

I look straight into his eyes, but my gaze is without challenge.

The King looks me up and down. His eyes narrow and then relax.

He runs his hands through his wavy dark hair, which is only now getting a few brushes of gray. He is not an unattractive man and I can see traces of Easton in him.

However, unlike Easton, there's a coldness emanating from him.

I don't want to admit it, but it fills me with fear.

"I have been watching you, Everly March," he says, adjusting himself in his seat. "And I like what I see."

"Thank you, sir."

"What do you think about this competition we are having here?"

That's a loaded question if I have ever heard one.

What do I think of kidnapping women for your pleasure?

What do I think about the games you play with people's lives?

Nothing good, I can tell you that.

But, of course, I can't.

I have to be diplomatic, but more than that actually.

I have to be charming and disarming.

I suspect that he's one of the judges, so it would behoove me to get him on my side.

"It's quite challenging, sir," I say, standing up straight and lifting my chin. "But I like a good challenge."

He looks at me for a moment. My heart sinks at the thought that I might have said something wrong.

But then he starts to laugh.

A loud roaring sound emanates from the pit of his stomach.

"I like being right, Everly. Even though I'm the King and people tend to agree with me, I like finding those moments in life when I and everyone else knows that I am right."

"Yes, sir," I say with a respectful nod.

"Well, at first, I thought that maybe I was being a little cruel with my son, Easton. I mean, he's kind of a tender soul. Not like my other son, Abbott."

The mention of Abbott's name sends shivers down my spine. "So, when it came time for me to punish Easton for raising his hand to his older brother to protect you..."

Punish Easton? What is he talking about? I narrow my eyes for a moment, but then force myself to relax them.

No, I can't let him see me question him.

But the King doesn't notice a thing.

"As you know, you are a commoner in these parts, and Easton is a Prince. That means that Easton had no right to hit his brother to protect you from him...no matter what Abbott does."

I stand before him, motionless.

"Do you not agree?" he asks, raising his eyebrow.

I feel myself starting to tremble in fear, but I remain stoic.

Unreadable.

"Of course, I do," I finally say.

"I thought you would." He laughs. "You're a smart girl. You may not know the rules of York quite yet, but you've got a good sense of how we do things when you were...down below."

My cheeks get flushed.

He knows.

Of course, he knows.

How could he not?

My heartbeat starts to speed up, and I take a deep breath to calm down.

I can't let him see me flustered. I can't let him rattle me.

"So, I guess, you agree with me then, huh?"

"About what, sir?" I ask quietly.

"That I made the right decision."

"I am sure you did." These words come out even quieter than the ones before.

He is toying with me.

Not quite revealing his whole hand.

Making me guess.

But what is he getting at?

"Good, that's good!" the King says, clapping his

hands. "And I thought that you might be upset by the fact that I had ordered Easton to spend the night with you."

What does that mean? A hundred different questions run through my mind. I look up at the King, no longer able to keep my true feelings to myself.

"Oh, you didn't know?" the King asks mockingly. "Well, yes, of course, you didn't know. I also ordered him not to tell you." He laughs again and his loud ugly laugh echoes around us.

"Don't look at me like that, honey. I didn't have a choice. Easton had to learn a lesson."

Fighting against everything that's boiling up within me, I'm somehow able to restrain even one tear from escaping my eyes.

"You know, I really thought you would have a harder time with this," the King adds.

"No, I understand, sir. You had to do what you had to do," I say loudly.

"I am glad to hear that. You might make a good Queen after all."

Good Queen?

What does that mean?

"You may go now." He waves his hand.

"Excuse me, but what do you mean by that, sir?"

I ask. Mirabelle tries to drag me away, but I turn to face him.

"I am looking for a new wife," the King says, giving me a coy smile.

I'm stunned. I stare at him, dumbfounded.

Mirabelle pushes me to get me to move.

"Let's go," she hisses. Reluctantly, I follow her out of the door.

"You knew about this?" I ask when we get outside.

"Please, follow me," she says instead.

"No, I will not!" I shrug her hand off my shoulder.

"I'm done doing what you tell me. I'm done with this place and these games."

Hot tears start to stream down my face. I try to hold them back, but I can't.

"Listen to me." Mirabelle spins me around. "You are not done with this place. You were great in there. Composed. Elegant. That's who you need to be."

"No," I mumble. "I can't."

"If you don't, then you will be sent back to the dungeons. Or worse."

"What's worse?" I ask through the tears.

"Sold off. To one of his friends. In another part of the world. You will never be heard from again."

I shake my head and collapse onto the ground. "No, no, no. I can't do this anymore."

Mirabelle slaps me across the face. This action stuns me and I look at her surprised.

"If you want to survive here, you have to stop feeling sorry for yourself. The King has taken a liking to you. That is not something that happens everyday. Trust me. You do not want to make him regret it."

"But what about Easton? How could he do that to me?" I ask. "I thought...I thought we had a connection."

"He was ordered to seduce you and make love to you. He was just doing as he was told."

I run my fingers over the gravel underneath my feet.

Less than an hour ago, I thought that I had met someone who really understood me.

Cared for me.

But perhaps not.

Perhaps that was all an illusion.

I look up at the sky and watch as the bright yellow moon moves behind a murky cloud.

Can I do this?

Can I survive this place?

I have to try.

What other choice do I have?

* * *

THANK you for reading HOUSE OF YORK!

I hope you enjoyed Everly and Easton's story.

Can't wait to find out what happens next?

One-click CROWN OF YORK now!

He used to be my only hope. **Easton Bay: a man who's as ruthless as he's gorgeous and as tender as he is cruel.** His every touch sends shivers down my spine.

I crave him.

He saved me once, but will he do it again? He's a mystery. An enigma. A suspense.

There's a darkness inside of him. It scares me to my very core. **Yet, I pull closer with each breath.** I am an addict and he is my drug.

What happens when it's not enough?

One-click CROWN OF YORK Now!

CONNECT WITH CHARLOTTE BYRD

Sign up for my **newsletter** to find out when I have new books!

You can also join my Facebook group, **Charlotte Byrd's Reader Club**, for exclusive giveaways and sneak peaks of future books.

I appreciate you sharing my books and telling your friends about them. Reviews help readers find my books! Please leave a review on your favorite site.

ABOUT CHARLOTTE BYRD

*C*harlotte Byrd is the bestselling author of many contemporary romance novels. She lives in Southern California with her husband, son, and a crazy toy Australian Shepherd. She loves books, hot weather and crystal blue waters.

Write her here:

charlotte@charlotte-byrd.com

Check out her books here:

www.charlotte-byrd.com

Connect with her here:

www.facebook.com/charlottebyrdbooks

Instagram: @charlottebyrdbooks

Twitter: @ByrdAuthor

Facebook Group: Charlotte Byrd's Reader Club

Newsletter

Made in the USA
Middletown, DE
07 August 2020